"DROOGS!" OWEN SHOUTED. "FLY!"

Nell didn't have to be told twice. She'd seen Droogs bring down a full-size Dragon!

"Fly, Beauty, fly!" Nell urged. Beauty stretched out her long white neck and Nell bent low. They sliced through the air like an arrow, quickly leaving Owen and his larger, slower dragon, Brahn, behind. Nell looked back and saw the flock gaining on Brahn.

A Droog leapt to Brahn's back and Owen turned and thrust at it with his dagger. It fell away, but two more quickly took its place. *Zap! Zap!* They tumbled to the river below like the first one, but more and more Droogs were closing in. Nell aimed her wand, stunning first one and then another, but there was no way she and Owen could keep up. Hundreds more were approaching!

"Fly, Nell!" he cried. "Save yourself!"

*"No!"* Nell shouted. "I won't leave you!"

"You have to!" Owen returned. "One of us has to survive, and I'm not going to make it!"

A spell! She needed to distract the Droogs somehow. Nell wracked her brain, trying to remember what she had learned about them from the Imperial Wizard's books.

# THE KEEPERS

## The Dragonling Series

By Jackie French Koller

## THE DRAGONLING COLLECTOR'S EDITION, Vol. 1

## THE DRAGONLING COLLECTOR'S EDITION, Vol. 2

Available from Simon & Schuster

# THE KEEPERS

## BOOK THREE: The Wizard's Scepter

By Jackie French Koller

ALADDIN PAPERBACKS
New York  London  Toronto  Sydney

If you purchased this book without a cover, you should be aware that this book is stolen property. It was reported as "unsold and destroyed" to the publisher, and neither the author nor the publisher has received any payment for this "stripped book."

This book is a work of fiction. Any references to historical events, real people, or real locales are used fictitiously. Other names, characters, places, and incidents are the product of the author's imagination, and any resemblance to actual events or locales or persons, living or dead, is entirely coincidental.

First Aladdin Paperbacks edition February 2004

Text copyright © 2004 by Jackie French Koller

ALADDIN PAPERBACKS
An imprint of Simon & Schuster
Children's Publishing Division
1230 Avenue of the Americas
New York, NY 10020

All rights reserved, including the right of reproduction in whole or in part in any form.

Designed by Debbie Sfetsios
The text of this book was set in Baskerville.

Printed in the United States of America
2 4 6 8 10 9 7 5 3 1

Library of Congress Control Number 2003107535

ISBN 0-689-85593-1

*To my sister-in-law, Julie, who, like all mothers,
is frequently required to be a wizard*

# Foreword

It is nearing the end of the First Chiliad[1] of the ancient time known as Eldearth. Graieconn, the Lord of Darkness, grows more powerful each day as the Imperial Wizard, Keeper of the Light, grows weaker. Soon, Graieconn hopes, the Scepter of Light, beacon of goodness, will be forever extinguished, and he will be able to rise from his underground prison to rule all of Eldearth. But all is not lost for the followers of the Light. An ancient prophecy promises a powerful new Keeper, but who will it be?

Despite the fact that he does not bear the prophesized Mark of the Dove, hope centers on Prince Owen, the son of King Einar of Xandria, but could the Promised One possibly be his twin sister, Arenelle? Arenelle does not bear the Mark either, and in the history of Eldearth, no girl has ever become a Wizard, let alone the *Imperial* Wizard, but Arenelle has proven that

---

[1] Thousand Years

she is no ordinary princess. She has completed the Wizard's Quest when all the other contenders have failed, and she has defeated her traitorous cousin, Lord Taman, and rescued her brother from the very clutches of Lord Graieconn. When the Imperial Wizard decrees that any would-be apprentice must first receive the Mantle of Trust from his or her father, King Einar is torn, and ultimately so is the mantle, for the king cannot decide who of his two children should receive the mantle. Instead he gives Owen and Arenelle half of the mantle and declares that it is up to one greater than him to decide. Now the time has come for Prince Owen to undertake the Wizard's Quest. Will he succeed as his sister has done, and if so, who will the Imperial Wizard accept as apprentice? Will the new apprentice be able to learn all he or she needs to know in time to save Eldearth?

# CHAPTER ONE

*Bounce! Bounce! Bounce!*

Princess Arenelle opened one eye and groaned.

"Oh, Minna, I'm so tired," she said to the little purple Demidragon who was eagerly bouncing on her chest. "It can't be morning yet."

Minna fluttered into the air and tugged back one of the bed curtains. A beam of light slanted in through the crack between Nell's window shutters.

*Odd,* she thought. The sun never shines in that window until afternoon. She rubbed her eyes and yawned. Everything ached—her legs, her back, her arms. She felt like she was one hundred years old instead of one-one. The events of the past week had taken a lot out of her.

"Graw?" said Minna, trying to tease Nell out of bed.

"All right, all right," said Nell, pushing back her quilts and getting up. "It's easy for you to be so bright-eyed and bushy tailed," she told the little Dragon. "You've been resting and recuperating these past few days while I've been tromping through Darkearth."

Minna zipped to the window and hovered. Nell walked over and pulled the shutters back.

"What the . . . ?" she whispered. The sun was already starting its descent into the west. How long had she been asleep? She turned and pointed at a small bell on her desk.

"Lady Fidelia," she said.

With a bright tinkle, the bell rose into the air and floated right through the wall and out of the room. Nell turned to Minna and smiled.

"No wonder you woke me up," she said. "You must be starving."

"Thrummm," said the little Dragon. She switched her tail back and forth eagerly.

Nell walked over to her desk and took several honey drops from a little crystal bowl.

"Here," she said, offering them to the Demidragon. "These will hold you over for a few minutes."

*Thwip, thwip, thwip,* went the little forked tongue, picking up the candies and slurping them into her mouth.

Nell poured water from the pitcher on her washstand into the washbasin and splashed some onto her face.

"That feels better," she said. She playfully flicked a little water at Minna, then laughed as the Dragon dove into the bowl and splashed her back.

"Enough! Enough!" she said, toweling off and ducking into her dressing room. She pulled on a simple blue frock.

"I've got to ask the seamstress to make me some trousers like Owen's," she said. "They're so much easier to maneuver in."

A knock came on the door.

"Or maybe I'll just ask Lady Fidelia to conjure me some," she mused. "Come in!" she called.

Lady Fidelia, Grand Court Witch of the castle, bustled in bearing a tray heaped with fruit and pastries.

"I thought you might be hungry when you finally woke up," she said with a smile.

Nell's stomach growled at the sight of the food.

"I am!" she said, picking up a pastry and handing a cluster of grapes to Minna, "but why did you let me sleep so late? What time is it anyway?"

"It's half past one," said Lady Fidelia, "and I let you sleep because you were exhausted. You may be a very special young lady, but you're not Immortal, you know. You have to take care of yourself."

"Yes, yes," Nell said impatiently, "but there is so much to do. I must prepare to return to the Palace of Light and I need to speak with Father before I leave. How is Owen coming with the preparations for his quest?"

"He . . . uh . . . left this morning," said Lady Fidelia.

"Left!" Nell's eyes popped. "But I wanted to talk to him, to give him some advice, and . . ." She touched the ruby pendant that never left her neck, the enchanted necklace that her mother had left to her to guide and protect her. "I was going to let him wear the pendant."

"You were?" Lady Fidelia's eyes widened. "But . . . I thought *you* wished to be Imperial Wizard. Have you grown to care for your brother so deeply?"

Nell had to admit that her feelings for Owen were still confusing. Separated at birth they had only known about each other for a few weeks and had not known they were brother and sister until just a few days ago.

"I'm . . . still not sure what I feel for Owen," she said, "but I owe him a debt of gratitude. He loaned me the enchanted dagger, which our mother gave to him, to protect me on my quest. I don't know if I could have succeeded without it. It seemed the least I could do was return the favor."

"Even at the risk of hurting your own chances of becoming Imperial Wizard?" asked Lady Fidelia.

Nell sighed. "If Owen is meant to fulfill the prophecy, then that is as it should be," she said. "All I want is a chance to fulfill *my* destiny, whatever that may be."

Lady Fidelia nodded. "That is as your mother wished," she said. "She would be pleased at your concern for your brother, but I think he will be all right, even without the pendant."

Nell shook her head. "I hope so," she said. "The quest is dangerous and difficult. One needs all the help one can get."

"I'm glad you feel that way," said Lady Fidelia, "because Owen *has* helped himself to something of yours."

Nell's brows arched in surprise. "Something of mine?" she said. "What?"

"Your white Dragon," said Lady Fidelia.

# CHAPTER TWO

Nell stomped through the corridors of the castle with Minna zipping along behind and Lady Fidelia huffing and puffing in a futile attempt to keep up. When Nell reached the double doors to the throne room, two guards barred her way.

"I will pass!" she demanded.

"I'm sorry, Princess," said one of the guards, "but the king is in conference with some visiting heads of state. He gave orders that he was not to be disturbed."

"I don't care!" said Nell. She pushed past the guards and slammed the doors open. Minna fluttered after her, nose in the air.

"How dare you!" Nell shouted.

King Einar looked up, then frowned. "Arenelle," he said. "What is the meaning of this?"

"How dare you let Owen take Beauty?" Nell demanded. "She's *my* Dragon!"

"Arenelle, we will discuss this later," said the king. "I am in the midst of some important business."

"Not as important as this," said Nell. "Owen's cheating! Beauty knows the way to the Palace of Light. Owen is supposed to find it by himself."

King Einar rolled his eyes. He stood up and looked at the other men around the table.

"If you will excuse me, gentlemen," he said. "My daughter can be a bit headstrong at times. This will only take a moment." He motioned Nell to follow him into the library, then he closed the door.

*Scratch! Scratch! Scratch!*

King Einar opened the door again, and Minna zipped through.

"Pfft!" she said, glaring at him.

"Is it not enough that I have to put up with your intrusions?" King Einar snapped at Nell. "Must I be insulted by your little worm as well?"

"Minna is as angry as I am," said Nell. "Beauty is her friend too."

"Well, it's not like anyone is hurting Beauty," said the king. "Owen just borrowed her. That's all."

"In the first place," said Nell, "she's been through as much as I have these past few days and she was desperately in need of a rest. And in the second place, *Owen is cheating*!"

"Will you stop saying that?" asked King Einar. "He's doing nothing of the kind. He's simply using his wits.

7

If you will read the Articles of Apprenticeship once again, you will see that they simply state that a would-be quester must find the Palace of Light alone."

*"Alone!"* Nell emphasized.

"Yes, *alone,*" her father repeated, "as in *without the company of other Folk.* Nothing is said about a Dragon. In fact you had this little worm with you, did you not?"

"Well, yes," said Nell, "but—"

"Then I don't see what your objection is," said the king. "Everyone knows that once a Dragon has been somewhere once, it never forgets the way. It seems to me quite clever of your brother to use that fact to his advantage."

"Clever!" Nell was steaming. "*I'm* the reason Beauty knows the way. She was with me when she learned it. It's like he's stealing that knowledge from me."

"Oh come now, Arenelle," said King Einar. "I do think you're just jealous because your brother had the good sense to figure out an easier way to achieve his objective."

"Jealous!" Nell sucked in a deep breath and exhaled slowly to calm herself. "Don't you understand?" she said. "There's a purpose to the quest. You're supposed to learn from it. I learned a tremendous amount."

"Well, then," said the king. "You shall have the advantage, won't you, when it comes time to compete for the apprenticeship."

"No, I won't," said Nell, "because the Imperial Wizard is an old fusspot who thinks girls should stick to being Witches and he'll probably accept Owen the minute he lays eyes on him."

"Perhaps that's the way it should be, Arenelle," said the king. "I don't know why you're so bent on changing things. The world has functioned well enough up until this point."

"How can you say that?" asked Nell. "Eldearth is on the brink of extinction!"

"Only because the Imperial Wizard is ailing," said King Einar. "Once Owen is—"

"Don't you see?" said Nell. "You are already assuming Owen will be the next Wizard. Why did you even give me half the mantle? It was just an empty gesture, wasn't it? You knew all along the Wizard would take Owen over me."

King Einar rubbed his eyes tiredly.

"You exhaust me, Arenelle," he said. "What would you have me do? I can't call the boy back. He's surely there by now."

Tears of frustration stung Nell's eyes.

"It's not fair," she said. "I worked so hard."

King Einar stepped forward and put an arm around Nell's shoulders.

"Leave me alone," she said, pulling away.

"Arenelle, please," said the king. "Don't be angry with me. I can't bear it."

Nell did not answer. She just crossed her arms and stared out the window.

The king sighed. "We'll have to finish this discussion

later," he said. "I am in the midst of negotiations."

Nell turned. "What kind of negotiations?"

"Nothing that concerns you," said the king.

There was an edge to the king's voice that belied his words. Nell knew that most of Xandria's business dealings had to do with the Montue trade. For decades the Xandrians had raided the lands of their neighbors, the Hillkin, and hunted the prized Montue, selling the pelts at a premium to the other kingdoms of Eldearth.

"You're not negotiating new Montue contracts, are you?" she asked suspiciously.

King Einar flushed guiltily. "As I said," he repeated. "It does not concern you."

"Everything in Eldearth concerns me," said Nell. "Please tell me that you are *not* negotiating new Montue contracts."

"I cannot tell you that," the king said quietly.

Nell's eyes flew wide open. "But you mustn't!" she said. "I told you about the Montue. They are sacred to the Hillkin, and I promised we would stop hunting them."

"You had no right to make such promises," said King Einar.

"But the Hillkin saved my life," said Nell, "and Owen's, too. They turned against Graieconn to help us and they need us as allies now to protect them from Graieconn's wrath."

"Arenelle," said the king. "You do not understand the

ways of the world. Xandria needs the Montue trade. It is the source of all our wealth."

"Then we must find another source of wealth," Nell declared.

"Just like that," said the king.

"Yes," said Nell. "Just like that."

The king chuckled indulgently. "A country does not change its whole way of life overnight, Arenelle," he said. "Even if we wished to, such changes would take a long time to effect."

"But what of the Hillkin?" asked Nell. "The Montue roam *their* lands. Their pelts should enrich Hillkin coffers. What right have we to take them?"

"The right of might," said King Einar simply. "We are stronger."

Nell's mouth dropped open. "But," she said, "that's wrong!"

"You are young and naïve," said King Einar. "In time you will grow old enough to understand the workings of Eldearth."

"I will never grow *that* old," said Nell.

The king turned away. "I must go," he said.

"Wait," said Nell. "What of Miette and Gurit and their kind? Were you just humoring me yesterday when you said you would look into their plight?"

Miette and Gurit were physically and mentally challenged Xandrians. Nell had met them on her journey to Darkearth and learned a shocking truth. In Xandria such Folk were typically left out at night, as infants, to be carried away by the Night Things and presumably killed.

"No, I was not humoring you," said King Einar. "I *will* look into it, when I have time."

"When will that be?" asked Nell.

"I don't know," said the king.

"What kind of answer is that?" Nell demanded.

"Arenelle," said King Einar impatiently. "Eldearth is in turmoil. The Dark Forces are wreaking havoc. I have much on my mind."

"But you still have time to sell Montue," said Nell.

"Yes! To raise more money for the army," the king boomed.

Nell huffed. "Then why did you promise me you would look into it?"

"I will take the matter under consideration," said the king, "but I can't pledge any quick remedies. Folk like your two friends have special needs and require more care than most Xandrians are equipped to give."

Nell stared at her father in disbelief. "They also have special minds and hearts and abilities," she said. "Without Miette and Gurit, Owen and I would probably be dead by now."

"I know that," said the king with a sigh, "and that is why I will look into it. I just can't make you any promises."

Nell shook her head. "I thought I knew you all these years," she said. "I thought you were a kind and loving man."

"I am a ruler first, Arenelle," said the king, "and a man second."

"It would seem to me that it should be the other way around," said Nell.

"And that is why I told you, and why I still believe, that you are not destined to be Imperial Wizard," said King Einar. "Your heart is too soft, Arenelle."

# CHAPTER THREE

Lady Fidelia was pacing outside the library when Nell and Minna emerged.

"I told you he would not take kindly to being interrupted," she said when she saw Nell's face.

"I don't care what he does or doesn't take kindly to," Nell said shortly. "He is no longer my father."

Lady Fidelia's jaw dropped.

*"What?"* She gasped. "You can't mean that he has disowned you?"

"No," said Nell. "*I* have disowned *him*." She stalked off in the direction of her chambers.

"Now, Princess," said Lady Fidelia, hurrying to keep up. "You can't mean that. You're just overwrought."

"Don't patronize me, Lady Fidelia," Nell snapped. "I mean precisely what I say. Please go and let Galen know that I will be needing a Dragon immediately, then come to my chambers so that you may conjure me some trousers."

"Trousers?" mumbled Lady Fidelia.

"Trousers," Nell repeated firmly.

Lady Fidelia shrugged helplessly. "As you wish, my lady." With a dip of her head she took off for the stables.

Nell stomped into her dressing room, her blood still boiling. She began flinging pieces of clothing out into the bedchamber.

"Men!" she raved. "It's no wonder Eldearth is in such a state! I'll show *him* whose heart is too soft. The world could do with a bit of softening if you ask me!" She turned and nearly tripped over a pile of clothes.

"What the . . . ?"

Just then Minna zipped into the dressing room, proudly carrying the skirt Nell had just flung out. She dropped it at Nell's feet and switched her tail excitedly.

Nell smiled in spite of herself. "I'm not playing fetch, Minna," she said. "I'm trying to pack."

"Graw?" said Minna, looking so disappointed that Nell picked up a shoe and tossed it for her.

"Thrummm," sang Minna, darting after the shoe.

Nell gathered up the pile of clothes Minna had collected and carried it out to her bed.

She paused in front of the painting of her mother. It smiled for her.

"Did you know of these injustices, Mother?" she asked. "How did you tolerate them?"

*Clunk.* A shoe bounced off her head and landed on the floor. Nell looked up and saw Minna hovering above her.

"Very funny," she said. Nell dropped the clothes onto the bed, and Minna scooped up the shoe and added it to the pile.

Absentmindedly Nell tossed it for Minna to fetch again.

A knock came on the door.

"Princess?" It was Lady Fidelia.

"Yes, come in," said Nell.

Lady Fidelia entered. "The Dragon will be ready when you are, Princess," she said, "but . . ."

"But what?" asked Nell.

"Must you leave so soon? I've hardly had a chance to speak to you since you've been back."

*Clunk.* The shoe dropped in front of Nell. She picked it up and flung it through the open window. Minna zipped after it.

"I'm sorry, Lady Fidelia," she said, "but I really have no choice. The longer I delay, the more likely the Imperial Wizard will appoint Owen as apprentice, and I can't let that happen."

Lady Fidelia looked confused. "But you told me just a short while ago that it didn't matter which of you were chosen," she said. "What has changed your mind?"

"Men!" said Nell emphatically.

"Meaning?" said Lady Fidelia.

"Meaning that men and Wizards have been running things far too long," said Nell. "I thought perhaps I could get Father to listen to reason, that maybe I could influence him to make changes, but he has turned a deaf ear to my pleas. No doubt Owen would do the same if he became Imperial Wizard. Men are a bunch of pigheaded fools, Lady Fidelia."

"Hey, you're being a little tough on us, aren't you?" said a voice.

Nell turned around. Minna had returned, but this time without the shoe. Instead an Imp was riding on her back.

"Pim!" cried Nell delightedly. "How are you?"

Minna landed on the bed, and Pim swung his splinted leg over her back and gently slid down.

"Well, I thought I was doing all right until I found out I was a pigheaded fool," said Pim.

Nell laughed. "You know I didn't mean you," she said. "You're not like *him*."

"Him?" asked Pim.

"Father," said Nell. "He makes me so mad, Pim. He is insensitive to the plight of Folk like Miette and Gurit, he refuses to stop hunting the Montue, and he has no plans to ally with the Hillkin."

Pim shook his head. "That's not good news," he said. "The Hillkin have angered Graieconn by helping us escape. They need your father on their side now if they are going to survive."

"Will you talk to Father, Pim?" Nell asked. "Maybe he'll listen to you."

"I'll try," said Pim, "but I don't think he's got a lot of respect for Weefolk."

"More than he does for Womenfolk, I'll wager," said Nell.

"Try not to be too hard on your father, Arenelle," said Lady Fidelia. "He believes that he is a just ruler and that what he does is for the better of the majority."

"But that's not good enough," said Nell. "There has to be justice for all, not just for the majority."

Lady Fidelia smiled.

"You are young," she said. "Your ideals are high. Your father had high ideals too once, but time has slowly chipped away at them."

"Well, nothing's going to chip mine away," Nell declared. "Now, if you'll conjure up those trousers for me, I'll be on my way."

"So soon, Princess?" asked Pim. "You've hardly had time to catch your breath. I was rather hoping you wouldn't leave for a while."

Nell smiled. "You mean, long enough for your leg to heal?"

Pim shrugged bashfully. "Something like that," he said. "We're a pair, you and me. Remember?"

"I remember," said Nell. "But I can't wait for you to get better, Pim. We have to be apart for now; you here trying to change Father's mind, me at the Palace of Light trying to change the Imperial Wizard's."

Pim nodded reluctantly.

"Okay," he said, "but you stay out of trouble. You hear?"

Nell grinned. "Trouble? Me?" she said innocently.

# CHAPTER FOUR

Brahn, Owen's Ring-necked Dragon, was slower than Beauty, but he was large and strong enough to make the whole trip without stopping to rest. Nell had made the trip several times now, so she knew the way, or most of it anyway. When she got confused, she just sent Minna a mind picture of the Palace of Light and let her take the lead for a while. It was dusk when they soared over the mountains and descended into what looked like a lake. This time Nell wasn't surprised when they broke through the lake's surface without getting wet and saw below them the glittering Palace of Light. The trip had passed quickly, her mind preoccupied with the argument she'd had with her father. Their parting had been a frosty one, and Nell's emotions were in a muddle. She had always loved and admired her father so much. It was hard to accept that he had tumbled off the pedestal she had placed him on.

As soon as Nell landed Brahn in the palace yard, a joyful cry sounded from inside the stable.

"Beauty!" Nell shouted.

"Thrummm!" cried Minna. She zipped over and darted through an open window. Nell led Brahn over to the stable and pushed open the door. A long white neck arched over one of the stalls. Beauty's lovely lavender eyes were lit with joy.

"Grrrummm," hummed the beautiful albino.

Nell ran and jumped up onto Beauty's stable's gate and threw her arms around the yearling's neck. Beauty nuzzled her head against Nell's back.

"You look fit enough," said Nell, pulling back and examining the Dragon critically. "I was so worried. I'll never forgive Owen for taking you like that."

Minna flitted around Beauty's head, planting tiny kisses on her shining white cheeks.

"Well, look who's here," said a voice.

Nell turned to see Zyphyra, the Imperial Wizard's feisty house Sprite, standing in the stable's doorway.

"Zephy!" said Nell. "Good to see you again."

"Why are *you* back?" Zyphyra asked shortly.

"To contend for the apprenticeship," said Nell.

"Too late. We've already got one," said Zephy, her chin in the air.

Nell's mouth gaped open. "What?" she cried. "What about me?"

"Sorry," said Zyphyra with a toss of her hand. "The apprentice has been chosen." Then she smiled flirtatiously and added, "and he's *cute,* too."

Nell frowned. "Being cute is not part of the criteria," she snapped.

"It is for me," said Zephy.

"Well, you're not the one making the decision, are you?" said Nell.

"I *told* you," Zyphyra repeated, "the decision has been made."

"We'll just see about that," said Nell. She pulled her portion of the mantle from the Ring-neck's saddlebag. Then she gave Beauty a kiss on the nose. "I'll see you later, my Beauty," she said. "Minna, are you coming with me, or staying with Beauty?"

Minna, perched on her favorite spot upon Beauty's head, hesitated for a moment, but when Nell headed for the door, she quickly followed.

"You're wasting your time," Zyphyra called after them.

Lady Aurora, Grand Court Witch of the palace, answered the door herself. Her silky white hair drifted around her like a cloud, and her bright green eyes sparkled like emeralds.

"Princess Arenelle," she said with a warm smile. "How delightful to see you again."

"I'm glad somebody thinks so," said Nell. "Zyphyra always makes me feel about as welcome as a toothache."

Lady Aurora laughed. "Oh, you know Zephy," she said. "That's just her way."

"She said that the Keeper had already accepted my brother as apprentice," said Nell.

"She's right about that, I'm afraid," said Lady Aurora.

"But that's not fair," Nell protested. "He never gave me a chance."

Lady Aurora nodded glumly. "Yes. Well . . . you know the Keeper."

"Can I see him at least?" asked Nell.

Lady Aurora shook her head. "I'm sorry," she said. "He's busy with your brother and gave orders that they were not to be disturbed."

Minna fluttered up.

"Oh! Your little Demidragon is all healed!" she said.

"Yes," said Nell, holding her arm up for Minna to perch upon. "I owe the Keeper a debt of thanks for that, at least. Our Dragon Master was able to pull Minna through, but if the Keeper hadn't helped her in the first place, she never would have made it home."

"I'll tell him that," said Lady Aurora. "I'm sure he'll be pleased."

"I'd like to tell him myself," said Nell. "May I come in?"

"You never give up, do you?" said Lady Aurora with a droll smile.

"Lady Aurora," said Nell. "You are a Witch and a woman. I beg for your help. Don't let the Keeper dismiss me. You know in your heart that he does so purely because I am female. If you let him deny seeing me for that reason, then you are also denying yourself and all the other Witches and women of Eldearth."

Lady Aurora's smile faded and she nodded slowly. "All right," she said. "Follow me."

# CHAPTER FIVE

Nell followed Lady Aurora through the corridors of the palace. The walls were made of glass and crystal, cut into facets that resembled diamonds. Lights and colors bounced and swirled everywhere, and Minna darted about, chasing illusions of butterflies and tiny shooting stars.

Lady Aurora stopped before a silver door and rapped upon it lightly.

"This is the library," she whispered.

"Who is it?" a gruff voice called out.

"It is I, Keeper," said Lady Aurora.

"I said I did not wish to be disturbed," the Imperial Wizard returned.

"It is a matter of some importance, Keeper," said Lady Aurora.

"All right. Enter then, but be quick about it."

Lady Aurora pushed the door open and motioned Nell inside. Minna followed her cautiously.

"Not you again!" the Imperial Wizard said, groaning. He was seated in an armchair. Facing him, in a similar chair, sat Owen, who seemed only mildly surprised to see his sister.

The room they were in was softer on the eyes than most of the other glittering rooms in the palace. It was made of marble and pearl with untold volumes of books brimming from alabaster shelves. The ceiling was an illusion of a pale blue sky where actual white doves floated serenely. With a cry of delight, Minna zoomed up to play with them.

The Wizard rose from his chair, and Nell noted that he seemed frailer than the last time she had seen him. His back was bowed and his hands trembled, but his voice certainly remained robust.

"Lady Aurora!" he shouted. "Come in here!"

"Please do not chastise Lady Aurora," said Nell. "If anyone deserves your anger, it is I."

"I don't recall addressing you," the Wizard retorted.

The flock of doves dove down from the ceiling and started careening around the room with Minna in hot pursuit.

"If I waited to be addressed," Nell replied, "I would be standing here till I was as old as you."

The Wizard turned red with rage, and Owen put a hand to his mouth in an obvious attempt to hide his amusement.

"And you," said Nell, putting her hands on her hips and glaring at her brother. "What do you mean by stealing Beauty? You never completed the quest."

Owen shrugged. "I didn't steal her. I borrowed her," he said. "And as for the quest, I simply chose to complete it in the quickest, most practical manner available to me. What's wrong with that?"

"It's cheating," said Nell. She turned back to the Wizard. "He cheated, and you don't even care," she said. "What kind of Imperial Wizard are you?"

"Get out!" the Wizard blared, pointing a long, thin finger at the door. A dove landed on his outstretched forefinger.

"Aargh," the Wizard grumbled, shaking the bird away.

Owen shook with silent laughter.

"No," said Nell. "I'm not leaving."

"What . . . you . . . how dare . . ." the Wizard sputtered. Another dove landed on the top of his head.

"You gave me your word," said Nell, trying hard not to laugh, "that you would accept me as apprentice if I came before you bearing the Mantle of Trust." She lifted the mantle in both arms. "Here it is. Now abide by your promise."

The Wizard stared at the mantle, his face wrinkled with displeasure. The dove grabbed a wormlike hank of his wispy hair in its beak and started tugging.

"Get out of here!" the Wizard shouted, waving his arms in the air.

The dove flapped away, and the Wizard pulled out his wand. He pointed it toward the ceiling, but before he could utter a word, Minna zoomed out of nowhere and snatched it from his hand.

"Rrronk!" she screeched, obviously remembering the last time he had used it on her.

"Give that back, you wretched worm!" the Wizard bellowed.

Minna retreated to one of the higher bookshelves, the wand firmly clasped in both claws.

The Wizard looked at Nell.

"Make her give that back," he said.

"What about my apprenticeship?" asked Nell, still holding the mantle.

"It would appear," said the Wizard, "that half of your mantle is missing."

"So is his!" said Nell, pointing at Owen.

"That's irrelevant," said the Wizard. "We are speaking of the promise I gave to you. I never said I would accept you with *half* a mantle, did I?"

"That's nonsense," said Nell, now seething with anger. "It didn't seem to bother you that *Owen* only had half a mantle. Or that *he* didn't bear the Mark of the Dove. Or that *he* hadn't completed the quest. You still made him your apprentice. Why do you hold me to a stricter set of standards?"

"Because you are different," said the Wizard.

"Different," said Nell, "but not less capable." She called to Minna, and the little Demidragon fluttered onto her shoulder. The Wizard reached out for the wand.

"Not so fast," said Nell. She took the wand from Minna and pointed it at the Wizard.

The Wizard chuckled. "Obviously you are unschooled in the ways of wands," he said. "By pointing the wand, you activate its magic, but you also risk losing it to someone more powerful than you."

He stretched out his open hand toward the wand, and Nell felt a force tugging at it. She gripped the wand as tightly as she could, but it began to slowly slip through her fingers. With her other hand, she grasped her mother's enchanted pendant. It began to pulsate, sending a surge of strength through her body. Her hand clamped tightly down upon the wand, and she began a fierce tug-of-war with the Wizard. Owen watched, obviously fascinated.

Nell wracked her brain for a spell, something that would put the Wizard under her control without hurting him. Then she remembered a tickling spell that Lady Fidelia used to cast when Nell was young.

"Powers passed from Witch to Witch," she chanted, "make this Wizard itch and twitch."

"Ah! Ooh. Hee!" The Wizard started twisting and writhing and scratching.

Owen burst out laughing.

"Stop! St-st-stop!" screeched the Wizard, dancing around in circles.

"Thrummm!" sang Minna. She fluttered to the floor and started dancing around in crazy circles too.

Nell laughed. "Minna thinks it's a game," she said.

"Pl-please," the Wizard pleaded, gasping and scratching wildly. "I'm an old man! Ooh! Hee! Ah!"

"Accept me as apprentice," said Nell, "and I'll make it stop."

"I . . . I already . . . have . . . have an apprentice," the Wizard protested, puffing.

"Well," said Nell, pointing the wand directly at the Wizard's ribs and wiggling it around, "perhaps you should have two."

"Ah! Hee! Ah! All right! I accept you!"

Nell lowered the wand and smiled.

The Wizard sagged over a chair, breathing hard.

"So. When do we begin?" asked Nell cheerfully.

The Wizard straightened up and glared at her. "Now," he said. Then he swept his hand in a great arc. "You may begin by reading these books."

Owen and Nell looked up at the towering bookshelves.

"Which ones?" asked Nell.

"All of them," said the Wizard.

# CHAPTER SIX

Nell rubbed her stinging eyes. At her left were several stacks of books as high as her waist. Owen had a similar pile on the floor beside him. Minna, bored with the silence, was stalking a ladybug as it meandered among the towers of books.

It had been a long week, filled from dawn till dusk with studying, spell practice, potion preparation, and scepter training. Both she and Owen had gotten to the point where they could tolerate holding the scepter for several minutes at a time, but it showed no signs of glowing for either of them yet.

"In time," the Imperial Wizard kept saying. "In time."

But time was running out. The Wizard was growing ever more frail, and the Light dimmer. Reports came in daily of new attacks on the various kingdoms of Eldearth.

Nell looked up at the shelves surrounding her on all four walls. Owen snapped his book shut and groaned.

"Do we *really* need to know every single detail about every single creature in Eldearth?" he complained.

"I know," Nell agreed. "The Keeper says knowledge is power, but it's been a week and this is as far as we've gotten. We'll be a hundred years old by the time we finish reading all these books."

"Mmm," Owen concurred. "And meanwhile the Dark Forces are out there wreaking havoc. If the pace doesn't pick up around here, it won't matter *who* becomes Imperial Wizard. It will be too late to do any good anyway."

Nell sighed. Owen's words were troubling and true. How were her friends faring, she wondered? The oppressed Cerulean women, the desperately ill little Arduan girl, the Hillkin, and so many others . . .

"I just hope Castle Xandria can withstand any attacks that may come in the meantime," said Owen.

Nell's eyes widened. "Castle Xandria?" she said. "Why would Graieconn attack Castle Xandria? We're no longer there."

"No, but Father and Lady Fidelia are. What better way to get to us than through them?"

Nell felt her heart squeeze. She'd been too consumed with anger at her father to think about his safety. She hadn't even tried to contact him since arriving at the palace. What if even now he was in danger . . . or worse?

"I must go and get my speaking star," she said. "I've got to see if they're okay."

"Don't worry," said Owen. "I contact Father and Lady Fidelia first thing every morning. There have been no attacks as of yet."

Nell bristled. "What business have you to be calling *my* father," she blurted.

Owen frowned. "He's *my* father too, remember?"

"I . . . I know," Nell sputtered, "but he's been my father longer. If anyone should be calling him, it's me."

"Hey," said Owen, "nobody's stopping you. And furthermore, he's been my father for as long as he's been yours. Don't think you've got any special claim on him just because you've had him to yourself all these years."

The library door burst open and Zyphyra flew in, blowing a sharp note on her flute.

"Wand practice," she said, "and you get to use real wands today! Follow me."

"Yay," said Owen, jumping up from his seat, "it's about time!" His book fell to the floor with a heavy thud.

"Rrronk!" cried Minna, staring at the book in dismay.

Owen bent over and lifted it slowly, then winced as he saw the squashed ladybug.

"Sorry about your playmate there, Minn," he said, scratching the little Dragon's head. "I'll make it up to you somehow."

"Pfft," said Minna with disgust.

"Come on, Minna," said Nell, calling to the little Dragon. "We'll find you someone else to play with."

Zyphyra drifted in a slow circle around Owen.

"Ready, cutie?" she asked.

Nell rolled her eyes.

"Lead on," said Owen, following the Sprite out through the door.

Nell stomped after them, sticking out her bottom lip. "The nerve of that boy, Minna," she whispered, "playing up to Father and Lady Fidelia! Especially when he knows things are icy between Father and me. It's not enough that he's the favorite of the Imperial Wizard and Zyphyra. Does he have to charm everybody?"

"Pfft," Minna repeated.

"*You,* at least, are a good judge of character," Nell whispered.

Zyphyra led them out to the palace garden where the Keeper was waiting, leaning heavily on his walking stick. Though there was not a cloud to be seen, the sky was a troubling color of slate blue, and the sun was as pale as a newborn chick.

Beauty and Brahn were grazing in an overgrown pasture on the other side of the stables. With a cry of joy, Minna zipped off to join them.

"Ah, there you are, my boy," said the Wizard. His voice was feeble, but animated. It was evident that he had grown quite fond of Owen.

"Keeper," said Owen with a dip of his head.

Nell waited to be acknowledged, but as usual the Wizard went right on as if she were invisible.

"This is the wand I started out with when I was an apprentice," the Wizard said, holding out a sleek silver wand with a white tip. Owen took it in his hands and gazed at it appreciatively.

"I am honored, Keeper," he said.

"Good, good," said the Wizard amiably. "Let's give it a whirl then, shall we?"

"What about me?" asked Nell.

"Let's start by making something disappear," said the Wizard.

"What about me?" said Nell a little more loudly.

The Wizard turned to look at her.

"Excellent suggestion," he said. "How good of you to volunteer." He turned back to Owen. "So then, let's start by making your *sister* disappear."

*"No!"* said Nell. "I meant, what about *my* wand?"

"Oh," said the Wizard. "Pity. I liked the other idea better."

Nell scowled. "My *wand*?" she repeated.

"Yes, of course," said the Wizard with a droll smile. "Zephy, my girl," he called. "See if there's another wand in the Magic case, please."

"Yes, Keeper," said Zyphyra. She zipped over to a black, velvet-covered box on the ground near the stables. A moment later she zipped back.

"Here," she said, holding out something that looked like an old leather Dragon whip, drooping and frayed.

"That's a wand?" said Nell.

"It is," said the Wizard. "Now, can we get on with the lesson, or have you something *else* to complain about?"

Nell grimaced and took the wand.

"All right then," said the Wizard, turning back to Owen. "See those apples I've placed on the fence? Start with the one on the right and repeat after me."

Owen pointed his wand.

"Should I do the left?" asked Nell.

"Yes, yes, whatever . . ." said the Wizard, shooing her away like a fly. "Now, my boy, do you remember the disappearing spell?"

Owen nodded. "Spirits of the shining light," he chanted, "hide this object from our sight."

The apple grew paler, but was still very much there.

"Concentrate, my boy," said the Wizard, "concentrate."

"What about me?" asked Nell.

The Wizard turned and looked down his thin nose at her. "What *about* you?" he asked.

"Should I try now?" Nell said.

"Yes, yes, go ahead," he said with an impatient nod. Then he turned back to Owen. "Try it again, my boy," he said.

Nell huffed. As usual, the Wizard was not about to offer her any guidance.

Owen squinted his eyes, focusing intently on the apple. "Spirits of the shining light," he said, "hide this object from our sight."

The apple became translucent, but still did not disappear.

Nell held her wand out. She concentrated as hard as she could.

"Spirits of the shining light," she said, "hide this object from our sight."

Nothing happened.

Owen gave her a smug smile and pointed his wand to the apples again. He took a deep breath and gritted his teeth, his face turning red with effort.

"Spirits of the shining light," he repeated, "hide this object from our sight."

The apple disappeared.

"Yes, yes!" The Wizard clapped his hands. "Very good! Very good indeed!"

Nell clenched her teeth, narrowed her eyes, and pointed her wand again. She summoned all her energy.

"Spirits of the shining light," she said, "hide this object from our sight."

Nothing happened.

Zyphyra burst out laughing.

Nell gave her a sidelong glance. "What's so funny?" she asked.

"I think you need to pay closer attention to where your wand is actually pointing," said Zephy.

Nell held her wand up and examined the warped, drooping point.

"Um . . . don't you feel a draft?" asked Owen.

Nell looked down and gasped.

Her trousers were missing!

Owen snickered, and the Imperial Wizard hid an amused smile behind his hand.

*"Keeper!"*

Nell looked up to see Lady Aurora rushing out of the palace. "I fear there is troubling news from Xandria!" she cried.

# CHAPTER SEVEN

"Banshee attack?" the Imperial Wizard repeated. "But it's high noon!"

Nell and Owen exchanged worried glances.

"Yes, Keeper," said Lady Aurora, "it is unusual for Banshees to venture out in broad daylight, but I assure you it is true. I have just received a star message from Lady Fidelia. She said it was a surprise attack, led by Lord Taman."

"Lord Taman!" Nell gasped. "I thought he was still a prisoner of the Hillkin!"

"I fear he has escaped, Princess. He is growing ever more wily, coming into his full power as a Wizard and Sorcerer."

Owen scowled at Nell. "I told you—"

"Never mind what you told me," Nell snapped. Then she shook her head in bewilderment. "I cannot believe," she blurted, "that Lord Taman, my own cousin, would turn against Father, his loving uncle, who has shown him nothing but kindness."

"Do not try to make sense of it, Princess," said Lady Aurora. "Graieconn trains his spies to be most persuasive, then sends them among the Folk of Eldearth to seek out the weak and vulnerable and entice them with promises of power and riches. Sadly Lord Taman was probably but a youth when Lord Graieconn's henchmen gained his ear, possibly still grieving for his lost parents."

Nell's heart went out to her wayward cousin. "I never thought of it that way," she said. "If only I could talk with him. Maybe I could—"

"Don't be a fool," said Owen coldly. "Taman's grief is long past. It is *greed* that motivates him now."

"The boy is right," said the Imperial Wizard. "No matter how evil gets a hold of a person, once it takes command of that person's soul, there is no turning back."

"But perhaps it's not too late for Lord Taman," Nell argued. "Perhaps some small part of his soul is still intact."

Owen rolled his eyes. "Are you forgetting our little *dinner party* with the Oggles?" he asked.

Nell sighed. It *had* seemed that Lord Taman had every intention of handing her and Owen over to the bloodthirsty Oggles only a few weeks back. But who knew? Would Lord Taman have had the stomach to go through with it if the Hillkin had not thwarted his plan?

"I will continue to hold out hope for his salvation,"

she vowed, "until I know for sure that hope is futile."

"Fine," said Owen. "You can stay here and fret over the soul of Lord Taman if you wish. I'm returning to Xandria to see if I can help Father and Lady Fidelia."

"Not without me, you're not," Nell declared.

The Wizard shook his head. "Neither of you is ready to fight yet," he said.

"I've been fighting ever since I was born," said Owen.

"And I already defeated a Banshee once," said Nell.

The Wizard looked at her incredulously. "Oh come now," he said.

"Believe me or don't," said Nell. "Either way, I'm going."

"Me too," said Owen.

The Wizard threw up his hands. "Headstrong—the two of you," he muttered. "Very well then. Get your-selves killed if you insist. Fetch their Dragons, Zyphyra."

"Princess!" said Lady Aurora suddenly. "What hap-pened to your trousers?"

Nell blushed. She had forgotten that she was still standing there in her underdrawers.

"I accidentally made them disappear," she said.

Lady Aurora put a hand to her mouth and chuckled. She pulled her wand from her sleeve pocket. "Let me help," she said, quickly rattling off the appropriate spell.

"Thank you," said Nell when her trousers reappeared.

Zephy flew across the yard, leading the two Dragons,

both saddled and ready to fly. Minna was perched atop Beauty's head like a little purple crown.

Owen looked up at the Wizard. "Can I take the wand?" he said. "I know I haven't had a lot of practice, but I've memorized dozens of spells."

The Wizard nodded. "All right," he said, "but use it with great care. They will do their best to take it away from you."

Nell looked down at her shabby wand. Was it even worth taking?

Lady Aurora must have read her thoughts.

"Give me that thing," she said, grimacing at the Wizard. "That should have been burned years ago. Here." She held out her own wand. "Take mine."

Nell's eyes widened. "Are you sure?" she asked.

"Lady Aurora," said the Wizard sternly, "your wand is very powerful. I do not think it wise–"

"I must respectfully disagree, Keeper," said Lady Aurora. "I think it only prudent that the princess have all the help she can get if she is to go up against the forces of Graieconn."

"But it would be extraordinarily dangerous if your wand were to fall into the wrong hands," the Wizard objected.

"These are times," said Lady Aurora, "that call for extraordinary measures."

The Wizard shook his head firmly. "It's too risky," he said. "I forbid it."

Lady Aurora put her hands on her hips. "In the first

41

place, my lord," she said, "the apprentice wand is almost as powerful as mine, and you gave it to the boy without hesitation, even though he is no more experienced than she. In the second place, you know that a Witch's wand is a very personal thing, and no one—not even you—has the right to tell her what she can or cannot do with it. Therefore I must respectfully refuse to comply with your order."

The Wizard glared at Lady Aurora. "Do you see what she's done?" he said, pointing at Nell. "Coming around here with all her impertinence! Now she's poisoning your mind!"

"She's not poisoning my mind," said Lady Aurora. "She's just giving me the courage to use it."

"Argh!" grumbled the Wizard. He whirled around and stalked away.

"What if you need the wand while I am gone?" Nell asked Lady Aurora.

"I will send Zyphyra to the Elves straight away and ask that they forge me a new one," said Lady Aurora. "I won't be without one for long."

Nell nodded. "Thank you," she said, humbly accepting the wand. "I will take good care of it."

Lady Aurora smiled. "I know," she said.

Owen had already mounted Brahn and was waiting for Nell. She hurried into her saddle as well.

"Keeper," Lady Aurora called out. "Have you the strength to transport them by Magic?"

The Imperial Wizard stopped and looked over his

shoulder. "Don't know why I should," he grumped.

"Because time is of the essence," said Lady Aurora sternly, "and you know it's the right thing to do."

The Wizard scowled, but turned and shuffled back over to the group. He stretched his hands out to touch both Dragons. "Spirits of the Ancient Ones," he chanted quietly, "spirits of the Yet-to-Come, speed these travelers on their way. Send them safely home this day."

There was a great roaring sound, and Nell, Owen, and the Dragons found themselves inside a whirling wind tunnel. Then, in what seemed to be just a matter of seconds, the wind subsided, and they emerged from the tunnel in the midst of a terrible rainstorm. Nell squinted through the pelting rain, but she could hardly see where they were.

"No wonder the Banshees are out at noon!" Owen shouted over the noise of the storm. "It's nearly dark as night! I can't make out anything through this driving rain!"

Lightning suddenly ripped across the sky.

"There, in the distance!" said Nell. "I can see the turrets of the castle!"

"What's that sound?" asked Owen.

Nell listened hard. Goose bumps crawled up her back. "Folks screaming and Banshees wailing," she said.

They both spurred their Dragons on, though the sky had turned darker.

A few moments later, another bolt of lightning

illuminated the village. A fierce battle was under way. Soldiers and townspeople—Humans, Witches, and Wizards—were side by side, battling the Banshees.

"Down, Beauty!" cried Nell, and the five companions dove from the sky, and into the battle.

# CHAPTER EIGHT

It was bedlam. Banshees closed in on them as soon as they neared the ground. Beauty and Brahn screamed and flamed, keeping the creatures at a distance. Minna dove at any that came close, belching fire and scratching at their filmy blackness.

Nell didn't know which way to turn. Rain poured down in sheets and lightning flashed. Folk were running and screaming. Many lay wounded. Wizards and Witches were plying their wands, and soldiers were wielding swords, but to no avail. The Banshees were larger and stronger than any Nell had ever seen.

Lord Taman was in the midst of the melee, shouting orders, and dueling with a number of valiant Witches and Wizards who were trying desperately to subdue him. He met each of their volleys with massive energy bolts of his own, laughing maniacally whenever one of them hit its mark.

"You never knew, did you?" he shouted with glee.

"Never knew that *I* was the most powerful Wizard in all Xandria!"

Beauty and Brahn fought wildly, flaming at as many Banshees as they could, but the sheer numbers were staggering.

"Look!" cried Owen, pointing. "It's Father!"

Nell looked. Their father was fighting hard, surrounded by a halo of whirling Banshees.

"Nell! Owen!" King Einar shouted, gasping. Two Banshees held him in a stranglehold. They seemed to be growing larger in size by the minute.

Nell slid from her saddle and pulled out her wand, but instantly a filmy hand clasped it and a jolt of searing heat shot through her body. She nearly dropped the wand.

"Stand back," said Owen. He pointed his wand at the Banshee.

"Owen, no!" Nell cried. "It will—"

It was too late. Owen's wand flew from his hand, and another Banshee grabbed it. Owen went sprawling backward from the impact of the confrontation.

"Rrriiii!" screeched Minna as a black shape swooped over her. "Rrriii, Rrriii!"

Nell heard Minna's cries and watched as the shape drifted away with the Demidragon enveloped in its dark folds.

"Minna!" Nell shrieked. Panic washed over her as she and the Banshee continued to fight for her wand. She fiercely gripped the wand with both hands, but the

Banshee kept growing larger and larger before her eyes. The pain in her hands was intense! The Banshee was winning. The rain-soaked wand was beginning to slip through her fingers! She needed more power!

*Power!*

She wished she had a free hand to touch her pendant, but she didn't dare let go of the wand.

And then it hit her. *Power!* Knowledge is power! That's what the Keeper had drilled into them day after day this last week. What did she know of Banshees? How could she use it against them? She continued fighting with all her strength, wracking her brain at the same time, trying to recall what she had learned of Banshees in the Imperial Wizard's books.

Then she remembered. Fear! Banshees fed on *fear!* If only she could control her fear . . .

*Calm, calm, calm,* she told herself. Nell took a deep breath and tried to slow her racing heart.

"Calm, calm, calm," she said out loud. Then, to the Banshee, Nell shouted, "I'm not afraid of you! What are you anyway? Why, you're no scarier than a pile of old rags. You can't hurt me."

Was it her imagination, or had the Banshee's grip weakened?

"I'm stronger than you are," Nell went on. "You can't win! Go back to where you came from."

And then the Banshee began to shrink visibly.

Nell took another deep breath and went on talking calmly and bravely. The calmer she became, the smaller the Banshee became! At last it let go of the wand and was blown away by the wind.

She turned to Owen, who had regained his feet and pulled out his dagger.

"Owen!" she said. "They feed on fear!"

"What?" cried Owen.

"They feed on fear!" Nell shouted. "We read about them, remember? Calm yourself, and they're powerless!"

"Are you crazy?" said Owen. He turned and slashed at an approaching Banshee. There was a flash of light and a terrible shriek. The creature began to wither, sinking to the ground and shriveling like a decaying fungus. Soon it melted into a muddy puddle and disappeared. Another Banshee grabbed Owen from behind. He whirled to face it.

"You can't fight them all, Owen!" Nell cried. "I'm telling you, if we can just calm everyone . . ."

"You fight your way, I'll fight mine!" yelled Owen.

Nell shook her head in frustration.

"Nell!" came a choking cry. It was their father, still flanked by two huge Banshees. Nell fought through the wind and rain to reach his side. "Father, they feed on fear," she cried. "Control your fear, and they're helpless!"

"Aagh!" her father cried out, gasping.

"Please trust me!" Nell cried. "I know what I'm saying. Clear your mind of fear. Think of something calming, something you love!"

Her father closed his eyes and tried to slow his breathing.

"That's it." Nell grabbed his hand and held it in her own. "Calm. Calm," she whispered.

Gradually the two Banshees shrank until they were nothing more than wisps. With high thin wails, they, too, disappeared into the storm.

The king smiled at Nell, breathing hard. "I thought of you," he said. "They didn't stand a chance."

Nell smiled back. "Spread the word!" she said, "Hurry!"

The king took off in one direction and Nell in the other. "They feed on fear!" she yelled. "Sing! Laugh! Hug! Do whatever you can to give yourselves courage!"

The cry passed throughout the village. One by one the stronger villagers defeated their foes and joined hands, helping the weaker. Sustaining songs broke out. Folk hugged one another. Banshees withered.

Lord Taman, stilled locked in a duel with several remaining Wizards, began to shout angrily.

"What are you doing, you idiots!" he screeched at the Banshees. "Don't let these fools outwit you! Keep your heads!"

Nell raced back to help the Dragons, sending them fearless, calming mind thoughts until their attackers shriveled into fetid wisps.

Lord Taman defeated another Wizard, then tore away from the last two and began charging through the streets, kicking and flailing at the remaining Banshees, zapping them with small bursts from his wand.

"Rouse yourselves you sniveling weaklings!" he screamed. "You're stronger than them! Don't give in!"

Nell looked around wildly.

"Minna!" she called. "Minna!"

From a distance she heard an answering cry.

A hand reached out and grabbed her arm. It was Owen. "Where are you going?"

"Minna!" Nell cried, tearing away.

Owen started to follow.

"No," said Nell, tossing him her wand. "Go after Lord Taman! He's trying to rally the Banshees."

Owen caught the wand and raced off after Lord Taman.

Nell followed the sound of Minna's cry until she caught up with a huge Banshee in the Lanes. It had a frightened child by one arm and it had nearly doubled in size. Minna cried weakly, enveloped in its folds.

Nell threw her arms around the child.

"Don't be afraid," she told the little girl. "It can't hurt you if you aren't afraid."

The child looked up at her, eyes wild. Nell wrapped her arms tighter around the little girl and began to hum.

"Rrronk," cried Minna weakly. Nell concentrated while she hummed, trying to send Minna calming thoughts.

"Nell! Watch out!" shouted Owen.

Nell turned to see Lord Taman racing toward her,

a crazed look upon his face. He was lashing out at every Banshee he passed along the way, cursing and screaming and calling them the vilest names he could summon.

The little girl started to scream.

"No," whispered Nell. "Stay calm. The Banshee is weakening."

"Hold on you slobbering piece of slime!" Lord Taman was yelling. "Hold on or I'll turn you and all your kind into stinking swamp sludge!"

With a shriek of outrage the Banshee suddenly released both Minna and the child and flew at the approaching Lord Taman!

"What? What are you doing! Keep away from me, you filthy idiot!"

Lord Taman stopped in his tracks and started stumbling backward.

"I warn you, get away!" he cried, leveling his wand at the creature.

The Banshee gave out a great moan, and all the remaining Banshees rose up and began to swirl together into a great cloud.

"I warned you!" bellowed Lord Taman. He aimed a massive bolt of power at the Banshee. Instantly it disappeared, but into the great void it left behind, the huge cloud of Banshees streamed.

Lord Taman's eyes grew round and white. He turned and fled into the night, the whirling Banshee cloud hot on his heels.

Nell and Owen stood blinking in the pelting rain.

"What just happened?" asked Owen.

"I'm not sure," said Nell, a smile of relief beginning to curl her lips. "But I think we won."

Owen glanced left and right. Folk were standing in a great circle, holding hands, hugging and consoling one another. Even King Einar and his soldiers were congratulating one another. Every last Banshee was gone.

Nell heard a small "thrummm" and looked down to see the little girl cuddling a cooing Minna in her arms.

# Chapter Nine

Morning dawned pale and chilly. Despite his exhilaration over the defeat of the Banshees, King Einar was somber at breakfast.

"Word has come that the Dark Forces are planning raids on many of the outlying provinces," he said. "Graieconn is wise. He's trying to keep the kingdoms occupied on many fronts so we cannot amass a single army to march against his forces."

"What will you do?" asked Owen.

"I don't know." The king looked sad and weary. "Do we sacrifice the Folk in those distant villages, or do we spread ourselves so thin that we put all of our Folk at risk? How does one make such choices?"

Nell pondered these matters in silence. She was growing weary too. Weary of the unending, unanswerable questions. She remembered her father's words to her not long ago. *It is hard to be a good king.*

*Good.* What did that word mean? Who had the right

to judge? If her father decided to sacrifice the outlying villages, would those Folk think him *good*? If he chose instead to put the rest of the kingdom at risk, how many of his subjects would think him *good*? She remembered her harsh words to him about the Hillkin and her friends Miette and Gurit. Too harsh, perhaps? How would she fare as a king? As an Imperial Wizard? Would she be *good*?

"I don't see where you have a choice," said Owen, matter-of-factly. "You must use your forces to their greatest advantage."

King Einar nodded. "Yes, I know," he said. "But it is hard . . . so hard."

Owen shrugged. "It is as it must be," he said. "No use fretting over what can't be helped."

Nell bristled. "How can you be so cold?" she asked Owen. "We're talking about lives. How can you just declare that some lives are more valuable than others?"

"It's all in the numbers, my dear sister," said Owen. "Nothing personal."

"It's personal to the Folk who will die," Nell declared.

King Einar sighed. "No. Your brother is right, Arenelle," he said. "Owen is obviously a born leader. He does not let his heart rule his head."

"And why is that *good*?" asked Nell. "Maybe if more rulers used their hearts, fewer battles would need to be fought."

King Einar and Owen exchanged condescending smirks.

"Yes, well it's time we were going," said Owen.

"Argh!" Nell grunted. "Why does no one take me seriously?"

King Einar relented. "I'm sorry, my little jewel," he said. "I *do* take you seriously. Your ways of thinking are different, but I am learning that they can be effective. You saved many lives yesterday, including mine, and I am grateful to you for that. But don't leap to conclusions. One happy outcome does not mean the war is over. The evil we face is grave—too grave, I fear, to be tamed by your gentle ways."

"We shall see," said Nell, rising from the table. "We shall see." She called to Minna, who was on her perch by the fireplace, but Minna seemed preoccupied. She stared blankly into thin air, her head tilted to one side as if listening to something.

"Minna," Nell called again.

Still no reaction.

Nell walked over to the little Dragon and listened. Her eyes widened.

"Raechel?" she said. "Is that you?"

"Yes, miss," came a voice so weak it was barely audible.

"Who is Raechel?" asked King Einar.

"A little child that I met on my quest," Nell answered. "I gave her my speaking star so she could see Minna whenever she wished."

"Is the little Dragon all better?" asked the small voice.

"Yes, she's fine," said Nell. "How are you, Raechel?"

"Not so good, miss," said the child softly, "but it be okay. I'll be with my father soon."

Nell swallowed hard.

"Where is her father?" asked Owen, who had come up alongside Nell.

"He's dead," said Nell quietly.

There was a little cough.

"Better go now, miss," said the child. "I be *very* tired."

Nell fought back tears.

"You hold on Raechel, you hear?" she said.

There was no answer.

"What's wrong with her?" asked Owen.

"She is dying," said Nell. She turned to face King Einar. "She needs Bloodpox potion, Father," she said. "You must let me take some to her."

"Bloodpox!" King Einar said, gasping. He strode over and grabbed Nell by the shoulders. "You met a child with Bloodpox? Tell me she didn't cough or sneeze on you!" he said. "Tell me you did not go near her."

"I . . . was near her," said Nell, "but . . ."

"By the Scepter!" King Einar went white. "How long ago? Do you have a rash? Do you feel feverish?" He turned to Owen. "Run to Lady Fidelia," he said. "Tell her to bring a vial of Bloodpox potion right away."

Owen nodded and sped from the room.

"Father, it was weeks ago," Nell cried, finally able to get a word in. "I'm fine!"

Lady Fidelia rushed into the room a few moments later, a vial in her hand. Owen followed close on her heels.

"Has the rash appeared?" she asked, wild-eyed.

"No," said Nell. "I'm fine."

"Oh, thank the Light," said Lady Fidelia with a sigh of relief.

"I'm not going to take any chances," said King Einar. "Give her the potion, Lady Fidelia."

"But, sire," said Lady Fidelia. "It's been several weeks. I really think the danger is past."

"Can I take the potion to Raechel?" Nell asked.

"Raechel?" King Einar frowned. "Of course not. It's for you."

"But I have no rash. Raechel is the one who needs it," said Nell. "You'd just be wasting it on me. *Please* let me take it to Raechel."

"No," said the king. "It's out of the question. Now, drink it."

"If I drink it," said Nell, "will you give me another dose for Raechel?"

"No," said King Einar. "I forbid you to go anywhere near that child, ever again."

"Why?" asked Nell.

"Because she has the Bloodpox!" King Einar boomed. "You're lucky you didn't catch it and spread it to the whole kingdom."

"And besides the fact," Owen put in, "we have to get back to our training. There's no time to go traipsing around the countryside looking for one sick child."

Nell looked at her brother. "I suppose it's just a matter of numbers again, right, Owen?" she asked shortly.

Owen shrugged. "I'm sorry," he said, "but it is. Delaying our training to save one life could end up costing many more in the end."

Nell shook her head. "I can't think like that," she said. "Raechel isn't a number. She's a sweet little girl with a mother who loves her desperately." Nell turned to King Einar again. "Raechel's mother is heartsick," she said, "just as you would be if it were me who was ill! Have you no compassion?"

King Einar hesitated, staring at Nell a long moment.

"Of course I have compassion," he said at last, "but I cannot cure all the world's ills, and neither can you. The sooner you learn that, the better. Now drink."

"No," said Nell quietly. She crossed her arms over her chest. "Not unless you give me another dose for Raechel."

Owen shook his head. "I've had enough of this," he said. "I'm leaving. I'll meet you back at the palace whenever you decide to quit being so stubborn."

"Suit yourself," said Nell with a shrug.

"I think Father's right about you," said Owen. "I don't think you've got the head to be an Imperial Wizard."

"And I don't think *you've* got the heart," said Nell.

Owen stomped out of the room.

"Give her that potion *now*," the king instructed Lady Fidelia.

Lady Fidelia opened the vial and put it to Nell's lips, but Nell refused to open her mouth.

The king glared at her. "All right," he said, throwing his hands up in frustration. "Drink it, and I'll give you another dose! Just be sure you deliver it promptly, while you are still under the protection of the potion."

# CHAPTER TEN

Nell eagerly scanned the wide plains below her.

"We have to be in time, Minna," she said. "We just *have* to."

Minna's tail switched excitedly as she, too, watched for a sign of the Arduan camp.

They reached the foothills to the south of the plains, and Nell turned Beauty and headed her north again. Back and forth they went, back and forth, passing over village after village, keeping constant watch for the ragged little tent city where Raechel lived.

"There!" Nell shouted at last. She pointed to a cluster of sandy-colored bumps on the far side of a small lake in the distance. "I think that's it, Minna!"

Minna craned her little neck and began softly thrumming as Beauty winged her way across the lake.

"It is!" cried Nell. "It's the Arduan camp. Down, Beauty!"

Beauty spiraled down and landed on the lakeshore.

"Stay here, Beauty," said Nell, patting the white Dragon's neck. "Have some water and take a little rest. This won't take long." She slid to the ground and took off at a trot with Minna whirring overhead.

"Don't come any closer!" yelled a man who crouched beside one of the outer tents. "We be Arduans here."

"I know," said Nell. "I'm not afraid. I've come to see a child named Raechel."

"Don't know any child by that name," said the man.

Nell's heart sank. "But . . . she has to be here," she said.

The man shrugged. "Could be," he said. "There be lots of children here. I'm just saying I don't know her is all."

"Can I look for her?" Nell asked.

"Suit yourself," said the man, "but it be foolhardy to walk among the Arduan unless you wants to be an Arduan too."

"I'm not afraid," Nell repeated. She smiled at the man as she walked by, but it was hard to make herself look at him. He was so covered with sores.

"Rrronk," said Minna as if she sensed his pain.

"Come, Minna," said Nell. She held out her arm, and Minna flew down and perched upon it. "It's so sad, isn't it?" she said quietly as they walked among the tents. There were old and young Folk, even babies, all coughing and hacking, covered with the awful sores. Some hobbled about, others gathered in small groups, still others sat alone, hunkered down beside their tents, staring at nothing, their faces contorted with pain.

As she walked among them, the Arduans looked at her in astonishment.

"Don't you be afraid of us?" more than one asked.

"No," said Nell, stopping to ask this one and that one if they knew where she might find Raechel.

Little children looked at her wide-eyed. "You be so pretty, miss," a little girl said. "Your skin be so smooth, miss," said another.

At last a woman nodded in answer to Nell's question.

"Yes, I know Raechel," she said sadly. "She be in the death tent, miss." She pointed to one tent that was larger than the others.

Nell's heart lurched.

"The death tent?" she said. "She's not . . ."

"Don't know, miss," said the woman. "All them in there is near the end."

Nell started to run, but stopped as she neared the tent. The coughing and moaning from inside was heart-breaking.

"Rrronk," cried Minna again.

Nell reached up and stroked her. "I know," she said softly. "It is rrronk."

Inside, Arduans lay on pallets, some coughing and thrashing, some moaning pitifully, others deathly still. All were covered completely with sores. Other Arduans, who were less sick, moved among the dying, offering them sips of water, trying to make them more comfortable. Beside many of the children, sat adults, murmuring words of comfort or singing softly. Some held the smallest children in their arms, rocking gently. Were they parents, Nell wondered, or simply taking the place of parents who couldn't be there?

Nell moved quietly among the pallets, fighting back tears, looking for Raechel. At last she saw a small girl about the right age and size. Nell knelt beside her.

"Raechel?" she said softly.

The child's eyes fluttered open, then widened.

"Miss!" she said hoarsely.

"Yes," said Nell.

"And the little Dragon!" said the child. She lifted her hand as if to reach for Minna, but she was so weak that she couldn't raise it more than an inch or two from the pallet.

Minna flew to Raechel's side and gently nuzzled the feverish little face. The child smiled weakly.

"She be so cute," she said feebly.

"Don't try to talk, Raechel," said Nell, pulling the vial from a sack at her waist. "I've come to make you better. I've brought some Bloodpox potion."

"Bloodpox potion!" The woman on the next pallet struggled to sit up. "Please give me some! My husband will pay you! Please!"

*"Bloodpox potion!!"* several others shouted. Instantly the whole tent was in an uproar. Dozens of Folk began

crawling toward Nell, their hands out, begging. A mother clawed past the others.

"Please!" she said, holding out her dying infant, "please save my baby!"

"I can't," said Nell. "I only have—aagh!"

Someone had cuffed Nell hard in the side of the head and grabbed the vial from her hand.

"Come back!" Nell cried, but the thief was madly pushing his way through the pitiful crowd. Another man jumped on him, then another. There was a terrible struggle, then the vial flew into the air and landed on the ground with a sickening *clink*! It shattered and the potion oozed onto the dirt. Arduans fought to get near it, licking up the mud.

Nell stared, frozen in horror.

"It's gone . . ." she mumbled. "It's gone and now no one shall have it! What is *wrong* with you Folk?"

The Arduans turned anguished, guilt-ridden eyes to hers, and Nell knew her anger was wasted, misdirected. She should have known better. Owen was right. She hadn't used her head. How had she expected to come in here and save one person? This terrible scene wasn't the Arduans' fault. It was hers.

"I'm sorry," she said quietly. "I'm sorry." Then she looked down at Raechel. The child's eyes were merely slits. Her breathing was faint and raspy.

"It's gone, Raechel," she said sadly. "The potion is gone. I'm so sorry."

"Don't be sad, miss," said Raechel. "It be all right.

You must go now. This not be a good place for you."

"No," said Nell, taking the little blistered hand in hers. "I'm staying. Tell me your favorite lullaby, Raechel."

"It be called 'Rock My Sweet Baby,'" said Raechel with a little cough. "Do you know it?"

"Yes," said Nell sadly. "I know it well." She lifted Raechel's fevered little body into her arms.

"Rock my sweet baby," she began to sing softly. "Rock, rock my sweet baby child."

Raechel's eyes closed, her little body relaxed, and her lips curled slightly into an expression of peace.

Nell sang and sang until the small body went totally limp.

Minna gave a small whimper and nudged Raechel's still hand. The child was no longer breathing.

# CHAPTER ELEVEN

Before taking off again, Nell burned her clothes, bathed herself and Minna thoroughly in the lake, and dressed in a fresh outfit she had brought along. She realized now how fortunate she had been not to catch the Bloodpox on her first meeting with Raechel, or to pass it on to others. She herself was protected this time by the potion, but she wanted to take every precaution to be sure she did not carry the disease away from the Arduan camp.

Several hours later she arrived at the little village of Katahr. She dismounted and led Beauty through the narrow streets, keeping Minna tucked securely under one arm. The Katahr Folk eyed her curiously, and the men seemed keenly interested in the Dragons. Nell would be glad when her mission was over and her Dragons were safely away from there.

"Excuse me," she said to everyone she met. "I'm looking for a woman whose husband and daughter came down with Bloodpox some time ago. The little girl's name was Raechel. Can you help me?"

Most of the Folk shuddered and hurried away at the mention of the dreaded disease. Others just shook their heads and shrugged.

"Let me take your Dragon for you while you looks," said a man, putting a hand on Beauty's reins.

"That won't be necessary," said Nell.

"I think it will," the man said menacingly.

Nell slid her wand out of her sleeve pocket.

"No, it won't," she said, aiming at the man's hand and releasing just enough energy to give him a quick sting.

He dropped the reins and rubbed his hand.

"I just be trying to help," he said with a scowl.

"Well, thank you just the same," said Nell, pulling Beauty away and moving on with her questioning.

"Go to the midwife," a woman told her at last. "She would know if anyone do." She pointed up a hill to a little adobe house with a sign out in front.

Nell made her way up the narrow cobblestone lane and rang a small bell that hung just to the left of a sign. There was a shuffling from inside, and then the door creaked open.

"Aye?" said an elderly woman with kind eyes.

"I'm looking for the mother of a child named Raechel," said Nell. "The villagers thought you might know her."

"What d'ya want with her?" asked the woman suspiciously.

"I bring news of the child," said Nell.

"What sort of news?" asked the woman.

Nell dropped her eyes. "Sad news," she said.

The old woman sighed. "Well, it won't be unexpected," she said. "Come along then."

The woman stepped out of the house and led Nell up the street. She was broad and walked with a heavy, lumbering step.

"Mind you keep a close eye on those Dragons of yours," she warned. "The Menfolk hereabouts'd love to get them in the pits."

Nell held Minna closer and looked around nervously.

"Don't fancy the sport myself," said the old woman. "Just plain cruel if you ask me."

Nell relaxed a bit, glad to know she had an ally in the old woman at least.

"Y'don't talk much, do you?" said the woman.

Nell sighed. "The message I carry is a heavy burden," she said quietly.

The old woman nodded. "Ay. We've had too many of those 'round here of late," she said. "Too many. It be a hard world to bring babies into."

Nell nodded, thinking how much she had changed in the past weeks. Not long ago she would have blithely replied that she was going to become Imperial Wizard and make the world a better place. Now she wasn't so sure. Did she have the strength? Did she have the wisdom? Did she have the heart?

"Here we be," said the old woman, stopping before a

shabby little hut. She knocked on the door. A moment later, a young woman answered it, her face weary beyond her years, a little child hiding in the folds of her skirt.

"Someone to see you, Mara," said the old woman.

The woman looked at Nell in surprise, then she looked at Beauty and Minna and her mouth dropped open.

"The Dragon girl!" she said.

"What?" asked Nell.

"The Dragon girl," Mara repeated. "That's what Raechel calls you. You gave her the magic star."

Nell nodded. "Yes," she said. "That would be me."

"Come in, come in," said Mara. "I am so grateful to you. That star means so much to her."

"Go ahead," the old woman prompted. "I'll look after the big Dragon."

Nell hesitated and the old woman laughed.

"Don't trust me, eh?" she said. "Well, that's good. It be wise to be cautious, especially in these dark times. But I won't betray you. You can ask Mara here."

Mara nodded. "I'd trust Old Nana with my life," she said. "She be the kindest woman I know."

Nell nodded, handing over Beauty's reins. Then she carried Minna into the house. A little doe-eyed boy peeked out from behind Mara's skirts.

"Would you like to play with the little Dragon?" Nell asked him.

"Please, miss," said the little boy, forgetting his shyness instantly. He stepped forward and held out his skinny arms. Nell handed Minna over.

The little boy giggled. "She be so cute," he said.

A stab of pain shot through Nell's heart, and tears sprang to her eyes.

"He . . . sounds just like his sister," she said hoarsely.

Mara looked at Nell and her smile faded. An incredible sadness filled her eyes. "She's dead, isn't she?" she said quietly. "That's what you came to tell me."

Nell nodded grimly.

Mara bit her lip, and a tear slid down her cheek. She put her hand over her mouth and turned away.

"I'm so sorry," said Nell.

Mara's shoulders shook for a few moments, then she wiped her cheeks and turned back, her eyes shining wetly.

"It don't be like I didn't expect it," she said. "It just be that . . ." The tears spilled over again. "She was so sweet, so young."

Instinctively Nell reached out and put her arms around the woman. They both hugged and cried together for a while.

"Maman?" asked the little boy. He tugged on his mother's skirt and looked up at her worriedly.

Mara dried her eyes and straightened her back. She bent down and stroked her little boy's cheek.

"Maman be all right," she said. "I just be sad because Raechel has gone to be with Papa now."

"Will her words still come out of the air?" the little boy asked.

"No," said Mara. "Not anymore."

"Oh," said the child, hanging his head.

Nell went over and knelt beside him. She took out the silver speaking star.

"This is the magic star that sent Raechel's words to you," she said. "Would you like to keep it?"

The child's eyes lit up. "Can I send words to Raechel and Papa?" he asked.

"I'm afraid not," said Nell. "No Magic is that strong. But you can send words to anyone on Eldearth."

"To my granny?" the boy asked.

Nell looked up at Mara.

"She lives in Bethtay Village," Mara said.

"Then hold the star like this," said Nell, handing the speaking star over to the child, "and say 'Granny, Bethtay Village.'"

The little boy repeated the words, and soon the star began to glow. In its center appeared a smiling, white-haired woman.

"Granny!" cried the child.

The woman's head jerked up. "Jeb?" she said.

"Yes, it be me, Granny!" shouted Jeb. "The nice Dragon girl gave me a magic star so I be able to talk to you whenever I want."

Jeb went on jabbering breathlessly to his grand-mother, and Mara smiled.

"Thank you," she said to Nell. "I'll be ever grateful to you for all you've done."

Nell shook her head sadly. "No," she said. "I have failed terribly. I have come to beg your forgiveness."

"My forgiveness?" Mara gave Nell a puzzled look. "Whatever for?"

"I had a vial of potion in my hands," said Nell, "enough to save Raechel's life. But I made the mistake of letting the other Arduans see it. There was a riot and it was destroyed."

Mara gazed at her in wretched sorrow.

"That be hard to know," she said. Then she sighed deeply. "But it don't be your fault. You be but a child yourself, and it was brave and good of you to try and help. How came you by this potion? It be very rare."

"In my kingdom there is a small amount," said Nell, "kept in case of a new outbreak. Were it up to me I would bring it here where it is needed, but my father, the king, will not let it go."

"The king?" said Mara, her eyes opening wide. "Do you be a princess then? Forgive me. I did not know." She bowed low.

"Do not bow before me," said Nell. "I am no better than you, no better than anyone. I have all the riches life can offer, and yet I cannot save the life of a single child."

Mara reached out and touched Nell's hair gently.

"You gave that child joy," she said, "and you gave me and Jebediah joy too. Your gift allowed us to be with her, to comfort her in her darkest hours. That be worth more than riches to us."

"Thrummm," sang Minna.

Nell looked up. The little Dragon had discovered a lump of dough rising on the hearth. She hovered over it, her little tail eagerly switching back and forth.

Mara laughed. "The hour grows late," she said. "Jebediah and I would be honored if you would take supper with us and spend the night."

"Well . . . I don't . . ."

"Pleeease," cried little Jeb, jumping up and down. "The little Dragon can sleep in my bed!" He bent down so that he was eye-to-eye with Minna and grinned.

"Thrummm," said Minna, licking his cheek with her little forked tongue.

Jeb giggled. "She be so cute," he said.

Nell's heart melted.

"All right," she said. "I suppose we could use a good night's sleep."

# Chapter Twelve

In the morning Mara walked with Nell to the outskirts of town. Little Jeb skipped alongside, proudly carrying Minna. Old Nana had stabled Beauty for the night, but Nell had slept uneasily and was relieved to be getting both Dragons safely out of Katahr.

"I thank you again for all you've done," said Mara, "and above all else, for being with Raechel at the end."

Nell sighed. "It's not right that this disease still exists when there are ways to cure it," she said. "I pledge to you that I will do everything in my power to change that."

Mara smiled kindly. "You be but a child yourself," she said. "Do not take the woes of all Eldearth on your shoulders. They be too heavy a burden for one so young."

"I may be young," said Nell, "but I am no longer a child."

"Aar. I see that in your eyes," said Mara. "You have

an old soul, Arenelle of Xandria. It be a deep well of wisdom you draw from."

"Then I must have a hole in my bucket," said Nell with a wry smile, "because I make some awfully foolish mistakes."

Mara smiled at her fondly. "May the scepter light your path," she said as Nell climbed onto the saddle.

"And yours," Nell returned. She whistled for Minna, and Jeb reluctantly released her.

"Away, Beauty," Nell commanded.

Mara and Jeb waved, little Jeb chasing along in Beauty's shadow until Nell zoomed away across the plains.

Nell arrived at the palace in a somber mood, still mourning Raechel. Owen would be sharply critical of her handling of the Bloodpox potion, she was sure. And the weather didn't help. The sky was as dull and gray as a storm cloud, yet there were no storm clouds in sight.

"Strange," Nell mumbled to Minna and Beauty when she entered the palace stables. "I wonder where Owen's Dragon is?"

"Princess!"

Nell whirled to see Lady Aurora standing in the doorway.

"I saw you land," she said. "I hurried out to tell you."

"To tell me what?" Nell asked.

"It's Zyphyra," Lady Aurora said worriedly. "She never returned from Elvenlea. I fear something terrible may have happened to her."

"Did Owen go after her?" Nell asked.

"Yes," said Lady Aurora, "but I fear for him, too. He was supposed to call me by speaking star last evening, but I've heard nothing."

"Where is Elvenlea?" asked Nell.

"It lies west of Cerulea," said Lady Aurora, "and south of the Oldenwood."

"Cerulea!" Nell's eyes widened. "Cerulea is a dangerous valley. I was nearly trapped there myself during my quest."

"I know," said Lady Aurora, "but I never dreamed Zyphyra would have trouble. Sprites have always had freedom of the skies."

"That's true," said Nell, "but the Trogs and Kwarts there are forever at war. Perhaps she got caught in a crossfire."

Lady Aurora wrung her hands. "Oh dear," she said. "I do hope she's not hurt. She's a snippy little thing at times, but I am deeply fond of her."

"I'll go after her," said Nell, "but you must keep Minna here. One of the Trogs had his eye on her last time, and I'll have enough to worry about trying to find Zyphyra and Owen without having to watch out for her, too."

"All right. Come, Minna," said Lady Aurora.

Minna flew obediently to Lady Aurora's shoulder.

"Perhaps I should take her into the palace and give her some treats while you make your exit," Lady Aurora suggested.

"Good idea," said Nell. "I'll just feed and water Beauty, and then we'll be on our way."

Lady Aurora sighed. "I wish I could go with you," she said, "but the Keeper is gravely ill."

Nell glanced at the sky.

"Is that why it's so gray today?" she asked.

Lady Aurora nodded. "I don't know how much longer he can last," she said. "It takes all his strength to handle the scepter now."

"I'll be back as quickly as I can," said Nell. "Tell him he must hold on until I bring Owen back!"

"Owen?" Lady Aurora's eyes searched Nell's. "Have you accepted that he is the Chosen One then?"

"I don't know," said Nell. "Father thinks he's a natural born leader."

"And you?" said Lady Aurora. "I see many such qualities in you as well."

Nell shook her head. "I'm not so sure," she said. "I've made some awful mistakes as of late."

"And what leader hasn't?" said Lady Aurora. "If you can admit your mistakes and learn from them, then you will make a strong leader indeed."

Nell sighed. "We'll see," she said. "I don't feel very strong just now."

Lady Aurora smiled gently. "You're as strong a young woman as I've ever known," she said, "and I've known many, including your mother."

"My mother!" Nell's eyes went wide. "You knew Queen Alethia?"

"She wasn't a queen then," said Lady Aurora. "We were girls together at the Academy of Witchcraft. She was very strong, but I sense that you have the potential to be stronger."

Nell's hand went instinctively to the pendant about her neck. It pulsated with warmth. "She *is* my strength," Nell told Lady Aurora.

"Then together you must be invincible," said Lady Aurora.

"No one is invincible, Lady Aurora," said Nell quietly. "Least of all me. But I am willing to give all I am for Eldearth. I only hope it's enough."

Lady Aurora nodded. "I'd best return to the Keeper," she said. "May the scepter light your path."

"And yours," Nell returned.

# Chapter Thirteen

"Do you remember this place, Beauty?" Nell asked, staring down into the blue valley of Cerulea from a vantage point high up on a mountainside. The valley floor was shrouded in mist, but Beauty seemed to have no difficulty recognizing it.

"Rrronk," she said.

Nell nodded. "You were almost dead when I found you here," she said softly. "But don't worry. I'm not going to let the Trogs near you again." She led Beauty into a cave. "You wait here," she said. "If I need you, I'll send you a mind message."

Beauty cocked her head unsurely. "Rrronk," she repeated.

"Don't worry about me," said Nell. "I learned my lesson last trip through this valley. They won't catch me again." She reached into Beauty's saddlebag and took out a vanishroud and her wand. She pulled the vanishroud over her head, making herself invisible, then tucked the wand up her sleeve. Nell scouted about on the ground until she found a sturdy walking stick.

"I'll be back as soon as I can," she said to Beauty. "Stay out of sight."

The mountain trail was steep and rocky, but Nell was prepared this time. She used the stick to brace herself and avoided the slipping and sliding that had hampered her previous descent. She wondered about the friends she had made on her earlier trip, Talitha and Leah, and Leah's children. Had they managed to escape from Leah's cruel husband, Orson?

As Nell climbed farther down, she realized that it was not mist shrouding the valley, but clouds of dust hanging in the air. Her ears caught snatches of sounds. Soon the sounds grew louder, harsh and brutal. They were battle sounds!

The Trogs and Kwarts were fighting again. Battle Dragons clashed in midair and on the ground below them two armies waged war.

*Good,* thought Nell. *Let them fight.* They were too preoccupied to notice her sniffing around for signs of Owen or Zyphyra.

The fighting was clustered around the river that divided Trog territory from Kwart territory. Nell gave that whole area a wide berth and crept into the Trog village from the far end. The streets were deserted. She hurried toward Orson's house expecting, for some reason, that she would find Zephy and Owen there.

But no one was there. Not Owen, Zephy, Orson,

Talitha, Leah, or the children. The walled-in court-yard was empty. Nell peeked into the house. It was a shambles, furniture tumbled about, rotting food and filthy clothes strewn everywhere. And what was that stench? When she walked around to the Dragon cages, she saw the source of the smell. The cages looked like they hadn't been mucked out in weeks. The Dragons milled about ankle deep in dung.

Nell wrinkled her nose in disgust. Then her eyes went wide. A Great Blue Dragon had stepped aside and behind it stood a Ring-neck Dragon, just like Owen's! She walked over to the cage.

"Brahn," she said softly.

The Ring-neck turned toward the sound of her voice.

It was Owen's Dragon!

Nell lifted her cloak so the beast could see her.

"Grrrummm," Brahn rumbled, lumbering over to press his face against the bars of the cage.

Nell reached out and stroked Brahn on his nose.

"Where is Owen, Brahn?" she asked. "Where is your master?" She formed a picture of Owen in her mind.

Brahn turned and forced his way through the herd of milling Dragons until he reached the far side of the cage. He thrashed his tail fretfully and stared at something beyond the courtyard wall, down toward the center of the village.

"Is that the way they took him?" Nell asked.

Brahn turned troubled eyes to hers.

"Don't worry. I'll find him," she said, "and then I'll come back for you."

Nell gave Brahn one more reassuring pat, then donned her vanishshroud again and headed toward the village's center. The streets were oddly quiet and deserted with only the distant battle sounds breaking the silence. Nell wondered again about Talitha, Leah, and the children. She remembered how difficult their lives had been, how they had been virtual prisoners of Orson. They weren't allowed to leave their compound unescorted or to talk with other women. Talitha was a slave, forced to cook and clean and toil her days away, but from what Nell had seen, Leah's life hadn't been much different. All women were treated like slaves in Cerulea.

Nell had given Talitha a vanishshroud in the hope that she could use it to escape, along with Leah and the children. Had they made it? Had they helped other women and children escape too?

Nell reached the village square. It was nothing more than a dusty common area with a stone well in its center, some broken down stocks, and—Nell shivered—a gallows platform. Surrounding the square were some ramshackle buildings, including a blacksmith shop, a meetinghouse, a Dragon stable, a tavern, and a jail.

A jail! Perhaps that was where she would find Owen and Zephy. Nell carefully crept up to the windows and peeked in. The building was as empty as Orson's house, and from the thick dust and cobwebs that covered everything, it appeared to have been so for some time.

"Look lively there!" someone shouted.

Nell whirled, but there was no one in sight.

"Faster, I tell ya!" the voice boomed again. "When the men gets back them'll have a powerful appetite and a bigger thirst!"

The voice was coming from inside the tavern next door. Nell crept cautiously closer. She peeked through a window in the back door and gasped. There, in the tavern's kitchen, were Owen and Zephy! They had shackles around their ankles, and a Trog, the tavern keeper Nell presumed, watched over them. The taverner had a pointed head and hairy arms like the Trogs Nell had met before, but his clothes were dark with grease and grime and his chin sported a scruff of gray beard.

Owen was stirring a huge vat of liquid and Zephy was kneading dough. Her beautiful wings were in tatters.

"Put some muscle into it, girl," the Trog demanded. He prodded Zephy with a wooden spoon. She knocked it away.

"Touch me again and I'll put some muscle into you!" she snapped, balling her right hand into a fist.

The Trog threw his head back and laughed, showing a mouthful of crooked, yellow teeth. Then he sobered and sneered.

"Good thing I be so good-natured," he said, growl-ing, "or I'd wrap ya up in that dough and bake ya fer supper."

Zyphyra just glared at him and went on punching and pushing the dough.

The Trog took a mug down from a shelf on the wall and walked over to Owen's vat. "Let me taste that now," he said, dipping the mug into the frothy liquid. He gulped it, spilling half the fluid down his hairy chest. "More joy pod!" he roared, whacking Owen on the back of the head. "Ya think us be a bunch of daisy sniffers here?"

Owen narrowed his eyes and reached into a sack on the floor. He crushed a handful of joy pods into the brew and began stirring again.

"More!" roared the Trog.

Owen repeated the request until the liquid began to bubble and hiss. The Trog dipped in another mug, gulped the liquid, then wiped his mouth and smacked his lips.

"Aar. That be more like it," he said.

Nell heard the rustle of wings and looked up. The battle Dragons were returning. She peeked around the corner and watched as, one by one, they set down in front of the stables next door. Their riders quickly dis-mounted, handing their beasts into the care of the Dragon Master, and making straight for the tavern. Soon the streets were filled with foot soldiers returning from the day's battle. Some straggled homeward, but most jammed into the already crowded tavern. Through the back door Nell could hear the tavern keeper barking orders at Owen and Zephy.

A side door in the stables suddenly opened, and a Trog came out into the alley where Nell stood. She gasped. It was Leah's husband, Orson, the cruel Trog who had captured her the last time she was in Cerulea!

# Chapter Fourteen

Nell held her breath, forgetting for a moment that she still wore the vanishshroud. When Orson took no notice of her, she softly exhaled in relief. He picked up a barrel and disappeared into the stables again, and Nell went back to spying on Owen, Zephy, and the tavern keeper.

Owen was dipping up mug after mug of the foaming joy juice, while Zyphyra ladled out bowls of steaming stew and sliced up heaps of bread and chunks of cheese. The tavern keeper dashed in and out of a swinging door that led to the dining room—out with trays heaped high with food, in with piles of dirty dishes. In between filling mugs Owen was elbow deep in a great tub, trying to keep up with the flow of dishes.

"Faster, faster, ya slackers!" the taverner bellowed.

Owen and Zephy already appeared on the brink of collapse. Their faces were red and shining with sweat. Their hair hung limply, stringing in their eyes, and their clothes were plastered to their backs. Zephy winced as she worked, as though she were in pain.

Nell carefully extracted her wand from her sleeve and backed away from the door, pointing her weapon at the window. She waited for the tavern keeper's next appearance. If she could just zap him enough to stun him for a few minutes, she could rush in and get Owen and Zephy out.

The swinging doors burst open once more and the tavern keeper strode into the kitchen. Nell took aim and channeled a burst of energy through the wand. Just at that second, the tavern keeper stepped aside, revealing a mirror-bright pot on the wall behind him.

*Zap!*

The wand flew from Nell's hand, and she was knocked head over heels backward into the dirt. The energy had bounced off the shining surface of the pot and returned to her. Nell had zapped herself!

"Oomph," she muttered, sitting up and rubbing her aching head.

"Well, well, well," said a gruff voice. "So, us meet again."

Nell looked up and found herself staring into the angry eyes of Orson. She realized too late that her vanishshroud had fallen off in her tumble.

"I . . . I don't know what you mean," she stammered.

"Oh yes ya does," Orson said, growling. "Yer the little snip that stole away me women, and me white Dragon, too."

"I'm sure you must be mistaken," said Nell. "I never . . ."

"Silence!" the Trog boomed. "Do ya take me fer a fool? Ya disappeared along with me Dragon and me women. Then bit by bit other women started disappearing, and children, too. It were you all right. Now tell me where them are."

"I don't know," said Nell.

"Well now. What be this?" said Orson suddenly. He bent and picked up her wand.

"That's mine!" Nell cried.

"Are it now?" said Orson with an evil grin. "So yer a Witch, is ya? No wonder ya pulled the fur over me eyes. Well, it won't happen again I tell ya."

"I'd be careful with that if I were you," said Nell. "It's a very powerful wand. It can be dangerous if you don't know how to use it."

"Aar. But you knows how to use it, don't yer? And yer going to teach me."

"I will not," said Nell.

The Trog reached down and grabbed the front of Nell's shirt and pulled her up until they were eye-to-eye.

"You'll do what I say, or you'll not live to see another day," the Trog bellowed into her face.

Nell twisted away from his reeking breath.

"Now, where did ya take me women?" he asked.

"I didn't take them anywhere. They ran away," said Nell.

"Ran away!" The Trog shook her until she faced him again. "That be a lie. What cause would them have ta run away?"

"Maybe it was your breath," said Nell, nearly swooning from the stench.

Orson shook her again. "Enough of yer sass!" he said. "Tell me where them are!"

*"I don't know,"* Nell repeated. "You can shake me till my brains fall out, but it won't make one bit of difference. I can't tell you what I don't know."

"Aargh!" Orson released her in disgust, then looked down at the wand. "Tell me how ta make a new one then," he said.

"A new what?" asked Nell.

"A new woman!" said Orson.

"No one can conjure another person," said Nell.

"I don't believe ya," said the Trog.

"I'm telling you, it's not possible," Nell insisted.

"And I'm telling ya it is!" Orson boomed. "Now make me a woman!"

Nell eyed him thoughtfully.

"All right," she said. "Give me the wand then."

The Trog laughed. "Do ya think I'm stupid?" he said. "Just teach me the spell. *Now!*"

"If you insist," Nell conceded, "but I'm warning you: It could be dangerous."

"I'll take me chances," said Orson.

"All right then," said Nell. "Circle the wand slowly around your head. Concentrate as hard as you can, picturing Leah in your mind, and repeat these words: Spirits of birth, spirits of life, make me a woman just like my wife."

Orson circled the wand around his head and repeated the words. No sooner did the word *wife* fall from his lips than there was a huge crackle and a great flash of light.

In Orson's place stood a female Trog that looked just like Leah!

Orson looked down at himself, or rather herself, and blinked in confusion.

"Ya tricked me!" she cried. "Ya made *me* a woman!"

"That's what you asked me to do," said Nell.

"That's not . . . what . . . huh?" Orson stammered, deeply bewildered.

Nell seized the moment to snatch the wand.

"Give that back!" Orson cried. "Ya has to change me back!"

Orson leapt at Nell, grabbing hold of the wand and knocking her down. The two rolled over and over in the dust, grunting and grappling, struggling for control of the wand.

Suddenly a great foot came down, pinning the wand to the ground and trapping Nell's fingers painfully underneath.

Nell looked up.

"Well, well, what does us have here?" asked the tavern keeper. "Looks ta me like two fresh wenches, just in time ta help out with the evening rush."

"I'm not a wench, ya clod!" yelled Orson.

"Yer not, eh?" said the tavern keeper with a wry smile. "Then I've been a bachelor too long. Where have ya been keeping yerself my pretty?" He bent down and pinched Orson's cheek.

Orson whacked his hand away.

"Get yer hands off me ya ugly beast!" she yelled.

The tavern keeper chuckled. "A feisty one," he said. "I likes that. And the customers will too. Come now." He yanked Orson to her feet and held her by the wrist. She twisted and fought to no avail, now smaller and weaker than when she was a male. The tavern keeper held her off with one hand and picked up the wand with the other.

Nell sat up, rubbing her sore fingers.

"And a Witch in the bargain," said the tavern keeper, shaking the wand at Nell. "Well, us'll just keep this in a safe place so ya don't get yer little self in trouble again, won't us? Now get to yer feet and be quick about it!"

# CHAPTER FIFTEEN

Owen and Zyphyra looked up. Both their jaws dropped as the tavern keeper pushed Nell and Orson through the door.

"You get over there and help out with them dishes," the keeper told Nell. "And you, my pretty." He patted Orson on the rear. "I wants you out front. Them men'll be mighty glad to feast their eyes on ya."

"I'm not a female I tell ya!" Orson protested as the keeper handed her a tray of brimming mugs. "It be me—Orson. You know me, Huslu. I'm Orson, the Dragon Master."

"Aar," Huslu said, chuckling. He gave Orson a wink and another pat on the rear. "Yer Orson, all right. Har!" He pushed her through the swinging doors, and an immediate chorus of whoops and whistles broke out in the other room.

Huslu pulled another set of shackles from a high shelf and snapped them around Nell's legs.

"Just in case ya had any thoughts about leaving," he said with a wry smile, "ya might be interested ta know that us takes a dim view of them that don't appreciate us's hospitality. Try to escape, and I'll make Dragon fodder out of ya." Then he picked up another tray of food and walked through the swinging doors.

"What are *you* doing here?" Owen whispered.

"Looking for you," said Nell.

"Well, you're a big help," Zyphyra put in. "What'd you go and get yourself captured for?"

"I might ask you the same thing," said Nell. "If you hadn't been foolish enough to get yourself caught, none of us would be here. What were you doing poking around in Cerulea anyway?"

"I wasn't poking around in Cerulea and I didn't get caught," snapped Zephy. "I got shot out of the air." She lifted her sleeve to show a bandage encircling her upper arm.

"Oh," said Nell awkwardly. "I'm sorry. Are you all right?"

Zyphyra shrugged. "I would be," she said, "if I could just get some rest."

Nell shook her head in disbelief. "What manner of creatures are these?" she asked, more to herself than anyone. "Who would shoot a Sprite? Sprites have always had the freedom of the skies, like birds."

"From what I can see," said Owen, "these Trogs have no honor and no use for any laws—even their own.

They do nothing but bicker and brawl, even amongst themselves."

"It's the wars," said Nell. "The women told me that the wars between the Trogs and the Kwarts have gone on for centuries. They don't even remember why they fight anymore. It's just become a way of life."

Owen nodded grimly. "And now we're caught up in it," he said.

"By the way, how did *you* get caught?" asked Nell.

Owen looked away. "Never mind. It's not important," he said.

"Of course it's important," Nell insisted. "We can all learn from one another's mistakes. How did you get caught?"

"I was . . . taking care of business," said Owen.

"What?" asked Nell.

Owen flushed. "Taking care of business," he repeated. "Isn't that what you said you call it? In other words nature called, and a Trog snuck up on me!"

"You mean you were . . ." Nell clapped a hand over her mouth to keep from giggling. Zephy snickered.

"It's not funny," said Owen.

"What about your wand?" asked Nell.

"A beast ate it," said Owen.

"What?" cried Nell. "How on Eldearth . . ."

"I dropped it in my haste to pull up my pants," said Owen, "and the Trog kicked it away from me and his pack beast scooped it up and ate it."

Nell bit her lip to keep from laughing. "You mean to tell me," she said when she had herself in control again, "that a Trog *and* his beast snuck up on you? Didn't you hear the beast?"

"Yes, I *heard* the beast," snapped Owen, "but I was crouched behind a rock, so I couldn't see it. I just figured it was Brahn milling around out there. Is that so hard to understand?"

"Um . . . no. I guess not," she said. "Have you still got your dagger at least?"

"No," said Owen.

"*No?*" Nell gasped. "Where is it?"

"The Trog has it."

"What Trog?"

"The Dragon Master."

"Orson?" Nell's eyes popped. "But the dagger is enchanted. I thought nobody could take it from you."

"He didn't take it," said Owen. "I gave it to him."

"You *gave* it to him?" Nell gasped incredulously. "Why, for goodness sake?"

"So he would take me to Zephy," said Owen. "He promised to help us both escape."

"And you *trusted* him?" Nell blurted.

Owen exhaled loudly. "Look who's talking, Miss Everyone-Ought-to-Use-Their-Heart-More-and-the-World-Would-be-a-Better-Place," he snapped.

Nell swallowed her retort.

"I think it was incredibly brave and generous of him

to make such a sacrifice for me," Zephy put in, gazing dreamily at Owen.

"Or incredibly stupid," Nell mumbled.

Owen stiffened. "And how did your mission of mercy turn out?" he asked sarcastically. "Did you find your sick little needle in a haystack?"

"Yes, I did, for your information," Nell replied hotly. Then her eyes filled with tears, and she looked away. "But I . . . made a foolish mistake and she died anyway."

There was a deep silence, broken only by the boisterous partying of the raucous crowd in the next room. When Nell looked back at Owen, he was gazing at her sadly.

"I'm sorry," he said.

Nell nodded and sighed. "Look at us," she said, "bickering like Trogs. We can't let their hate rub off on us. We've got to pull together, or we'll never get out of here alive."

"Aye," said Owen.

Zephy even gave off being contentious long enough to nod.

Just then Huslu bustled through the doors again with another mountain of dirty dishes.

"What's this?" he shouted. "What's going on in here? A tea party?" He put down the tray, picked up a mop, and started flogging them all. "Get to work! Get back to work, or you'll be Dragon fodder this night!"

# CHAPTER SIXTEEN

It was long after halfnight when the last Trog stumbled out of the tavern to go home and sleep off the night's reveling. In just a few short hours they would all be rolling out of bed again and dragging themselves off to the battlefield once more.

"What a life," Nell whispered.

Orson staggered through the swinging doors under the weight of yet another tray piled high with dishes.

"I've got blisters on my blisters," she grumbled, "and I've been pinched and poked and squeezed black and blue. Where's that blasted wand of yer's? Ya had better change me back!"

"The tavern keeper has it," said Nell. "Ask him."

Orson frowned and shook her head. "Him won't listen. Him thinks I'm daft."

"Then I guess you'd better get used to being a woman," said Nell.

"Never!" cried Orson. Then she yawned and leaned

heavily against the sink. "Somehow I'll figure something out. . . . Tomorrow."

Huslu came through the swinging doors. "Hurry up and finish them dishes," he said. "I wants ta get ta bed."

"Aar. Me too," said Orson. She put her tray down on the table and headed for the back door.

"Uh, uh, uh," said Huslu. "Just where does ya think yer going?"

"Home," said Orson. "I did the work ya asked of me. Now I needs some sleep."

"Oh, you'll get some sleep," said Huslu. "Right in here with the rest of the help." He pushed a side door open and revealed a tiny room with several narrow cots.

"But I have a house of me own," Orson protested. "I be the Dragon Master."

"Aar," said Huslu, "and I be a princess. Yer one confused wench! Now finish yer work, all of ya, so I can shackle ya to yer beds and get some sleep!"

"But I has rights!" Orson insisted. "Ya can't keep me here."

"Yer a wench! Ya has no rights!" Huslu shouted. "And I'm getting tired of yer whining!" He came over and slapped Orson across the face. "Now shut yer mouth and finish yer work!"

Nell lay awake trying to plot an escape. She longed to be able to talk to Owen and Zephy, but Orson's cot lay in between them. Sometime in the night Nell was surprised to hear a soft, sniffling sound from the next cot.

"Orson," she whispered, "is that you?"

"No," said Orson, but her husky voice gave away the truth.

"Are you hurt?" asked Nell.

"No," came the injured voice again.

"Look," said Nell. "I'm sure you think it's a sign of weakness to cry, but it's not, you know. My father cries sometimes and he's a king."

There was another sniff.

"We'll figure out some way to change you back," said Nell. "Don't worry."

"That not be it," said Orson.

"What is it then?" asked Nell.

"It be Leah," said Orson. "I treated her just like Huslu and them others treated me today. Worse sometimes. No wonder her ran away. No wonder them all ran away."

"That's a part of why they ran away, it's true," said Nell. "But there's more. Leah and Talitha told me the women are sick to death of the fighting, Orson. They say it has no point, that it's just become a senseless way of life. They want to raise their children in peace."

"The Kwarts will never let ther be peace," said Orson. "Them hates us."

"And you hate them," said Nell. "Somebody has to stop hating, Orson. Hate is like a Banshee. It feeds on fear. You hate the Kwarts because you fear that they will try and change your way of life. They hate you for the same reason. Cerulea is big enough for both peoples. You can live in peace here, together, respecting one another's ways, or you can fight and fight and fight until you wipe one another off the face of Eldearth. What makes more sense?"

"The hate already be too strong," said Orson. "Us can't get beyond it."

"Maybe if there were someone both peoples respected," said Nell, "someone who had no stake in the outcome . . . maybe if we could get your leaders to sit down with that person . . ."

Orson sighed. "Trogs and Kwarts won't listen to nobody," he said.

"Not even your women?" asked Nell.

"Least of all us's women," said Orson.

"Then someone has to begin, Orson. You're an important man here—the Dragon Master. If you listen, then maybe others will listen too. That's the way it has to start."

"But me women are gone," said Orson.

"If I can find them," said Nell, "will you listen to them?"

Orson raised herself up on one elbow. "Does ya think ya can?" she asked.

"Perhaps," said Nell. "I can at least try."

Orson considered a long moment, then sighed. "It aren't no use," he said. "Even if ya could find them, them won't come back. Why would Leah come back after the way I treated her?"

"Leah still has a soft place in her heart for you," said

Nell. "I know she does. I saw it when she spoke to me of how kindly you treated her when you were children, of how she grew to love you."

"Her said that to you?" asked Orson.

"Yes," said Nell. "I think, if I can find her, I can talk her into coming back."

Orson's eyes misted over. "If ya can bring me Leah home," she said, "I will listen. I swear it."

# CHAPTER SEVENTEEN

"Owen, Zephy," Nell whispered. "Wake up!"

Owen rolled over and looked at Nell.

Zephy sat up and rubbed her eyes. "What's going on?" she asked.

"We have to plan our escape," said Nell.

Owen and Zephy both cast wary glances at Orson.

"Orson is with us now," said Nell. "She's going to help."

"Why?" asked Owen suspiciously.

"None of yer business," snapped Orson.

"Orson," said Nell gently. "If you ever hope to get Leah back, you're going to have to learn to be honest about your feelings for her."

"Leah don't be here," said Orson shortly.

"No," said Nell, "but it's not going to be easy for you to tell her about your feelings after all these years. You could use some practice."

Orson scowled, then glanced at Owen awkwardly.

"I . . . misses me wife," she mumbled. "The Witch says her'll help me get Leah and me babies back."

Owen started to smile.

"Don't laugh or I'll mash ya in the mouth!" Orson snapped.

Owen's smile quickly vanished. "All right, all right," he said. "So how do we get out of here?"

"First of all, we've got to find my wand," said Nell, "and your dagger."

"And Brahn," said Owen. "I'm not leaving my Dragon here."

"Yer Dragon don't be a problem," said Orson. "Him's in me cages at home. If us can get out of here, I'll set him free. And yer dagger be right here in me boot. At least it were before the Witch made me a woman." She bent down and pulled up her skirt. "Aar, it's still ther!" She pulled the small dagger free and held it up. "Wisht I'da recalled that I had it. I'da given old Huslu something ta remember me by tonight."

"Maybe you still can," said Nell.

"What do ya mean?" asked Orson.

"He's got my wand," said Nell, "and we need to get it back."

Orson nodded. "That be for sure."

"All right then. Here's what we're going to do," said Nell. "Owen, you take the dagger and undo our shackles. Orson, you call Huslu down here and pretend like you're interested in him."

"Interested . . . how?" asked Orson warily.

"Romantically," said Nell.

Orson's eyes bugged out. "Oh no!" she said. "Forget that! I aren't making no play for no man!"

Nell smiled. "Fine then," she said. "Just stay a woman. I like you better that way anyhow."

Orson sucked in a deep breath and blew it out noisily. "All right," she said, "I'll do it." Then she looked around at all three of them. "But if any of ya ever breathes a word of this ta anybody, I'll hunt ya down and knock yer brains out if it takes me till the end of me days!"

Nell, Owen, and Zephy exchanged amused glances, trying hard not to giggle.

"Don't worry," said Nell. "Now, hurry. We've got to get out of here under the cover of darkness."

Owen undid all the shackles, then handed the dagger back to Orson. Orson lay down and pulled her thin blanket up to her chin. With a last tortured look at Nell, she cried out, "Oh, Huslu-u-u! Huslu can ya hear me? Huslu-u-u!"

After a few moments, there was a groaning of rope springs overhead, then the sound of footsteps on the stairs. The door creaked open, and Huslu peeked in, a nightcap on his head.

"What'da ya want?" he growled.

"I . . . I've just been layin' here thinking what a handsome man ya is," said Orson in a syrupy-sweet voice.

Nell bit her tongue, shaking with silent laughter.

"Ya have such strong muscles," Orson went on, "and such derstinguished gray hair."

Huslu pushed the door open a bit wider.

"Yer having me on," he said suspiciously.

"How can ya say that?" said Orson. "Surely ya knows how attractive ya are."

Huslu stepped into the room. He brushed back the hair on his cheeks.

"Well," he said, "the ladies has always sort of given me the eye."

Orson made a snorting sound.

Huslu stiffened. "What's that?" he snapped.

"Er, nothing," said Orson. "The dust from this old blanket be getting up me nose."

"Oh," said Huslu.

Nell reached out furtively and poked Orson in the ribs.

"A-As I were saying," Orson went on, "I just been laying here feeling lonely and thinking what a shame it be for me ta be all alone down here, and a handsome man like you ta be all alone up there when us could be . . . could be . . ."

"Could be what?" asked Huslu.

"Ya knows," said Orson flirtatiously. "Keeping each other . . . company."

Huslu straightened and cleared his throat. "Aar, well, it's true I does get lonely now and then too." He walked over to Orson's bedside. "Maybe ya has a point."

"I has a point all right," said Orson, jumping up and grabbing Huslu by the scruff of his beard. He pressed the dagger against the thick flesh of Huslu's neck. "I has a very sharp point," she said with a laugh.

# Chapter Eighteen

Nell sent Beauty a mind message, and the white Dragon was waiting for them, pacing nervously outside Orson's Dragon cages when they arrived.

"Rrronk!" Beauty cried as soon as she set eyes on Orson, restored now to his former fearsome-looking self.

"It's all right, Beauty," Nell said soothingly. "Orson is a friend now. He's had a change of heart."

"And a lot of other stuff too," said Owen with a laugh.

Orson narrowed his eyes. "None of that never happened—remember?" he said menacingly.

"Oh, right," said Owen. "Forgot about our bargain there for a moment."

"Forget again, and I'll have yer liver on a skewer," snapped Orson.

Owen nodded soberly, and Orson opened the cage that held Brahn and went in to get him.

"Orson may have had a change of heart," Owen whispered to Nell, "but it sure hasn't done much for his disposition."

"Patience, Brother," Nell whispered back. "Change takes time."

Orson harnessed Brahn and led him out into the yard.

"Which way does Elvenlea lie?" Nell asked Zyphyra.

"Through that fjord," the Sprite replied, pointing at a narrow passageway between the mountains.

Nell's eyes widened. "Really?" she said. "I think that's the way the Cerulean women went."

"Nar," Orson interrupted. "That be Droog territory. The women's wouldn't go ther."

"They would if they had protection," said Nell.

Orson's brow creased. "What kind of protection?" he asked.

"A Witch's protection," said Nell.

Orson's eyes narrowed. "I knew it were yer fault!" he said, growling.

"I just helped them leave," said Nell. "It was *your* fault they wanted to leave."

Orson frowned, but said nothing more.

Owen climbed onto Brahn's saddle, and Nell climbed onto Beauty's. Zephy approached Owen, and he put a hand out and quickly hoisted her up in front of him on the saddle.

"Zephy should ride with me," said Nell. "Our best defense against Droogs is speed, and Beauty's a lot faster than Brahn. You don't need any extra weight slowing him down."

"Extra weight!" Zephy huffed. "I'll have you know Sprites weigh next to nothing!"

"Maybe so," said Nell, "but next to nothing is still something."

"Hmph," said Zephy, crossing her arms. "That's nonsense. You're just jealous."

"Jealous of what?" Nell demanded. "Owen is my *brother*!"

"Enough!" Owen interrupted. "Will you two stop bickering? Time is wasting! Zephy will be fine with me."

Nell shrugged. "Suit yourselves," she said.

"Away, Brahn!" Owen cried, and the Ring-neck sprang into the air.

Orson touched Nell's ankle, and she looked down at him. He leaned in close.

"Tell Leah," he said quietly. "Tell her I . . . uh . . ." He cleared his throat and shifted awkwardly from one foot to the other. "Tell her I loves her," he blurted, then quickly looked away.

Nell smiled. "I'll tell her," she said.

Orson nodded awkwardly. "And take care," he added. "Them Droogs be dangerous."

Nell didn't need to be reminded. She'd tangled with the poison-fanged, razor-clawed creatures before. "I know," she said. "I will." Then she lifted the reins. "Away, Beauty!" she cried.

Beauty launched into the night sky, and the Trog village fell away below them. In a few seconds Beauty caught Brahn. The river below glinted in the moonlight like a silver pathway leading them straight to the fjord.

"I'm heading down low," Nell called out once they entered the pass. "I want to watch for signs of the women."

"You aren't serious," said Owen.

"Why not?" asked Nell.

"Because we have to get through this territory as fast as we possibly can," said Owen. "We've got no time for sightseeing."

"I'm not *sightseeing*," said Nell. "I'm keeping my promise."

"To a *Trog*?" Owen shouted incredulously.

"What's that supposed to mean?" asked Nell.

"It means that Trogs don't keep promises," said Owen.

"Or live by rules," Zephy added.

"So why should we honor promises to them?" Owen went on.

"Because I've gained Orson's trust," said Nell, "and he's agreed to listen to the women. If I don't keep my promise, he'll think I've betrayed him and nothing will ever change!"

"Who cares?" shouted Owen. "Let the Trogs and the Kwarts wipe each other out. Less trouble for the rest of us if you ask me."

"How can you think like that?" Nell asked.

"Because I'm practical," said Owen, "and if you ever hope to be a leader, you'd better learn to be practical too."

Suddenly there was a loud shriek, and Nell turned toward the sound. A huge flock of monkeylike creatures was winging its way toward them.

"Droogs!" Owen shouted. "Fly!"

Nell didn't have to be told twice. She knew how dangerous Droogs were—she'd seen Droogs bring down a full-size Dragon! She pulled out her wand, and Owen unsheathed his dagger, but they were clearly outnumbered. Their best hope was to outdistance the flock.

"Fly, Beauty, fly!" Nell urged.

Beauty stretched out her long white neck, and Nell bent low against the Dragon's body. They sliced through the air like an arrow, quickly leaving Owen and Zephy behind. Nell looked back and saw the black flock gaining on Brahn.

"Hurry, Owen, hurry!" she screamed.

"Brahn is flying as fast as he can!" Owen shouted.

"I told you Zephy should have flown with me!" Nell cried.

"This is no time for 'I told you so's!" Owen yelled. A Droog leapt to Brahn's back, and Owen turned and thrust his dagger at it. The Droog fell away, but two more quickly took its place. *Zap! Zap!* They tumbled to the river below like the first one, but more and more Droogs were closing in. Nell aimed her wand, stunning first one and then another, but there was no way she and Owen could defend themselves. Hundreds more were approaching!

"Fly, Nell!" Owen cried. "Save yourself!"

"*No!*" Nell shouted. "I won't leave you!"

"You have to!" Owen returned. "One of us has to survive, and I'm not going to make it!"

"Yes, you are!" shouted Zephy. With a sudden jerk she threw herself out of the saddle. She fluttered her tattered wings madly, but they wouldn't keep her aloft.

"Zephy!" cried Owen. "What are you doing?"

"Fly, Owen," Zephy cried as she slowly tumbled toward the river below. "I can't let you die!"

"Don't be an idiot!" Owen cried. He dove after her, but before he could reach her a pair of Droogs swooped down and snatched her in their claws. They zoomed upward with their catch toward their mountain caves.

"Zephy!" Nell cried. She reined Beauty around and tore after the Droogs. She tried to aim her wand, but the creatures were zigging and zagging madly.

A spell! She needed to distract the Droogs somehow. She wracked her brain, trying to remember what she had learned about them from the Imperial Wizard's books. They lived in caves and rarely ventured out in broad daylight. But that was when the light was strong, of course. They ate flesh of all kinds, but their favorite delicacy was fish.

Fish!

Nell looked down at the river below. It would take a

powerful spell, but she *had* to do it. She grabbed her mother's pendant and pointed her wand.

"Be with me, Mother," she whispered. Then she began to chant. "Water spirits, swift and deep, make the finned ones dance and leap. Send them high to catch the eye and lure the Droogs down from the sky."

The water began to churn and boil. Then a silver fish leapt into the air, then another and another! The river surface was teeming with leaping, twirling fish. The sound of their bodies slapping the surface rose like a thunderous applause.

With cries of exultation, the Droogs gave up the chase and zoomed down to partake of the tempting feast. Zephy's captors dropped her in midair and sped off. She flapped her ragged wings desperately, trying to slow her fall.

"Hang on, Zephy! I'm coming!" called Nell. "Faster, Beauty! Faster!"

Beauty stretched out her neck and raked at the air with her great wings. She dove down, down, snatching Zephy out of the air just before she tumbled into the teeming river.

Nell leaned over and looked at the Sprite, dangling precariously from Beauty's claws.

"You all right?" she asked.

"Yeah, but I could do with a little less excitement!" Zephy replied, gasping for air.

Nell smiled and patted Beauty's neck. "Good work, girl," she said. "Now up, gently." Beauty slowed and began to climb again. Before long, Owen and Brahn caught up with them.

"Zephy, you okay?" Owen yelled.

"Sure, I'm great," Zephy returned. "I think I'm going to take up Dragon-diving as a hobby."

Owen smiled. "Well, at least your sense of humor is intact," he said. Then he motioned to Nell. "I'm going to bring Brahn in under Beauty!" he yelled. "When I give the word, tell Beauty to let Zephy go."

Nell leaned over and watched as Owen maneuvered the Ring-neck in close enough to reach his arms up to Zephy.

"Now!" he yelled.

"Beauty, release!" Nell cried.

Beauty opened her claws, and the Sprite dropped neatly into Owen's arms.

"Nice work," called out Nell.

"You're not so bad yourself," Owen replied. "That was some pretty clever spell work!"

Nell smiled and looked down at the river below. "Thanks," she said. "I feel bad about the fish, though."

Owen rolled his eyes and thumped his chest. "Oh, yes, I feel *awful*!" he mocked.

Nell frowned. "How can you be so heartless?" she asked.

Owen shook his head. "They're *fish,* Nell," he said. "Toughen up a little, will you?"

# CHAPTER NINETEEN

At the end of the fjord the river cascaded down into a sparkling blue lake, and the mountains gave way to rolling green hills and wide vistas of meadow and woodland. Everything was so fresh and green that the land itself seemed to glow.

"Elvenlea," called Zephy, her eyes shining.

"What is that light?" shouted Nell.

"Goodness is powerful in Elvenlea," Zephy replied. "It is one of the last strongholds of the Light."

Out of the corner of her eye Nell noticed a thin plume of smoke off to their left. She craned her neck and saw what looked like a small campsite on the banks of the lake.

"Is that an Elf camp?" she asked.

Zephy looked.

"No," she said. "It's too crude for an Elf camp."

"Maybe it's the women, then!" said Nell.

"Perhaps," Zephy agreed.

"Owen," Nell called. "I'm going down to check it out."

Owen frowned. "I told you there's no time for that," he said. "We've got to get the new wands and get back to the palace as quickly as we can."

"You take Zephy and go ahead then," said Nell. "I made a promise that I intend to keep."

Owen gave his head an exasperated shake. "Lead on then," he called. "I'm not leaving you alone."

"Why not?" asked Nell. "I can take care of myself."

"There's no telling what we're going to encounter on the way back to the palace!" Owen shouted. "I'm *not* leaving you alone."

Nell shrugged. "All right," she replied with a wry smile, "but may I remind you that the last time we went our separate ways, it wasn't *me* who ended up in need of rescuing."

Owen grimaced. "Just lead on, Sister, dear!"

As Beauty flew low over the campsite, Nell saw a number of lean-tos and cook fires. Several pointy-headed Folk—some large, some small—moved about among the makeshift dwellings.

"It *is* them!" Nell cried.

Just then a familiar face looked up.

"Talitha!" Nell cried. "Talitha, it's me, Arenelle!"

Talitha's mouth fell open and she started running along the ground, in Beauty's shadow. When the Dragon touched down, the slave girl rushed up, breathless.

"I don't believe it!" she cried. "Ya said ya would come back, and here ya is! And look at yer Dragon. . . . Her really is a beauty, just like ya said!"

Nell slid to the ground and gave Talitha a big hug. "I told you so," she said with a laugh.

Brahn landed and Zephy and Owen dismounted. Zephy looked scratched-up and tired, but otherwise seemed in good shape.

"This is my brother," said Nell, "and my . . . friend Zephy." She glanced tentatively at Zephy, who smiled and nodded.

"Welcome," said Talitha. "Come, come. Us doesn't have much, but what be ours be yers." She led the three back to camp where the others waited.

"Why, it be our daft little friend!" Leah cried when she set eyes on Nell. The Trog woman sat on a log with her baby girl in her arms. Her little boy played in the dirt by her feet.

Nell bent down until she was eye-to-eye with the boy. "Remember me, Raja?" she asked. "Remember my little friend Minna?"

"'Ragon?" said the child, his eyes darting around excitedly.

"I didn't bring her this time," said Nell. "But I brought my big, white Dragon. Would you like to see her?"

"'Ragon!" said the child, scrambling to his feet.

"I'll take him," said Zephy, reaching a hand out. "You tend to your business, Princess."

"I'll help Zephy," said Owen, then looked around the clearing. "Any of you other children want to see the Dragons?" he asked.

With joyful shouts several other little Trogs hurried

116

over. Zephy and Owen herded them off toward the Dragons.

"Did I hear that Sprite call you 'Princess'?" asked Talitha.

"Yes," said Nell. "Didn't I mention that the last time we met?"

Talitha shook her head, her lips curling into a fond smile. "No," she said. "Yer just full of surprises, isn't ya? Come, sit with us." She gestured toward several logs that had been arranged in a circle. Nell sat on one, and the other women came over and gathered around her. Leah got up and put the sleeping baby in a basket that served as a cradle, then she returned to the circle. Once introductions had been made, Talitha smiled at Nell once more.

"So, what brings ya back to us?" she asked.

"I bear a message from Orson," said Nell.

Talitha gasped. "Yer been back to the valley?" she said.

Nell nodded.

"And ya spoke ta Orson?" Leah asked wide-eyed.

"Yes," said Nell.

"And lived ta tell of it?" Talitha put in.

Nell laughed. "Orson has had a change of heart," she said. "In fact he told me to tell you, Leah, that he loves you."

Leah pulled back and looked at Nell incredulously.

"Now I *knows* ya be daft," she said. "Orson never spoke them words since . . . since we was children."

"I'm serious," said Nell. "He wants you to come home. He has promised to listen to your concerns and speak to the other men."

"Yer having us on," said one of the other women. "Orson be one of the meanest of them all. Him has no sympathy fer women's cares."

"He does now," said Nell.

"Why?" asked Talitha suspiciously.

"Because he's been one," said Nell.

"Been one what?" asked Leah.

"He's been a woman," said Nell. "I changed him into one."

"You *what*?" Talitha gasped in disbelief.

"I changed him into a woman," Nell repeated.

"How?" asked Talitha.

"I'm a Witch," said Nell. "I suppose I forgot to mention that the last time too."

"Ya said something about being apprentice ta the Imperial Wizard," said Talitha, "but I thought yer was just . . ."

"A daft little thing. I know," said Nell with a laugh. "Well, I'm not. My mother was a powerful Witch, and with her help I'm finding I can do some pretty amazing things myself."

"Like change Orson inter a women?" said Leah, still staring at her in astonishment.

"Yes," said Nell. "He spent a night waiting on tables at the tavern, being pinched and grabbed and insulted by the men. Then the tavern keeper berated him more and slapped him across the face. He cried afterward—"

"Orson cried?" Leah exclaimed.

"Yes," said Nell, "not for himself, but for you. For the way he had treated you."

Leah sat back and rested her chin in her hand. "Well, I'll be," she mumbled.

Talitha crossed her arms over her chest. "I don't care how sorry him is," she said. "I'm never going back."

"Me neither," said another young girl. Several older women voiced their agreement.

"Look at this place," Talitha went on. "It be so peaceful here, and the Elves has said us can stay as long as us wants. Us can talk with one another here. Us are free ta laugh, ta sing, ta wear what us want, walk where us will. Why would us ever go back ta being prisoners in us's own homes?"

"Aar," said another woman. "And here us can raise us's children without hate. Why would us ever go back to the killing and war?"

"Because ther be women and children still there," said Leah quietly. "More than us can ever bring here. And because women are not meant to live without men, nor men without women. If us wants our Folk ta survive, us must go back."

Talitha shook her head. "No," she said. "Ther men won't listen. Nothing will change."

The other women murmured among themselves.

Leah looked at Nell. "Do ya believe Orson?" she asked. "Do ya think him is serious about speaking out?"

"Yes," said Nell. "I do."

Leah was quiet a long time, then she nodded. "Then I will go back," she said.

"Leah, no!" cried Talitha. "Even if Orson be serious, him's only one man. Others won't change."

"One man be a beginning," said Leah. "If me husband be willing ta stand up fer me, then I be willing ta stand by him's side."

"Leah be right," said another of the older women. "Running away made sense when it were us's only choice, but if ther be a chance that us can change things fer the other women, fer the other children, then us must go back."

"I'm not promising any of you that it will be easy," said Nell.

"No," said Leah. "It may not even be possible, but us won't know if us don't try." She looked over at Talitha. "Ya can stay here if ya like," she said. "Ya don't have children ta worry about."

Talitha chewed her lip for several moments, then she sighed. "Well, I'd like ta have children someday . . ." she said. "I guess it be my job to try and build a better world fer 'em."

One by one the other women reluctantly agreed.

Nell looked around the circle and smiled. "You're brave women," she said.

Talitha smiled too. "So are ya," she said, "ya daft little thing."

# Chapter Twenty

Owen and Zephy brought their young charges back, and Nell left the women to plan their journey home.

"I'll be back to see you when I can," said Nell.

"Ya take care of yerself," said Talitha. "Eldearth needs the likes of ya."

"Eldearth needs the likes of all of us," said Nell.

With a final farewell Nell followed Owen and Zephy back to where the Dragons waited.

"The Elfsmith can be found at Elvenlea Castle," said Zephy. She pointed to the west, then climbed up onto the saddle behind Owen.

The two Dragons took off and soared out over the green meadows and golden fields of Elvenlea. Nell was thoroughly taken by the enchanting beauty of the place. There were lush valleys and sparkling streams, thick wooded copses and silvery lakes. Herds of wild Unicorn roamed free, and wildlife of all kinds abounded. Tucked between the hills and dales were cozy hamlets and quiet farms.

At last in the distance the graceful spires of a castle rose. As they drew closer they could see that the castle formed the centerpiece of a large village. Nell, Owen, and Zephy landed just outside the village gates, where a single Elf stood guard.

Nell had never seen a real Elf before. This one was not tall, but not short either. He was actually very close to Nell's own height. He was slender and fair, with pale golden hair and very light blue eyes. He wore a tunic of green and seemed very much a part of the natural landscape. He held a tall bow in one hand and a quiver of arrows was strapped to his back. He seemed unconcerned about the approach of the strangers.

"Welcome to Elvenlea," he said in a soft musical voice. He bowed his head. "Xylon, at your service."

"We have met before," said Zephy with a polite dip of her head. "May I present Prince Owen and Princess Arenelle of Xandria."

The Elf dipped his head again. "My pleasure, your graces."

"We are come on an errand from the Palace of Light," Zephy went on. "Lady Aurora requests that a new wand be forged for her."

"And one for me as well, if you don't mind," said Owen. "I sort of . . . lost mine."

Xylon gazed intently at Nell and Owen, then nodded. "Follow me," he said.

As if by Magic the great gates opened, revealing the loveliest city Nell had ever seen. The buildings were so delicate—all arches and spires and filigree carvings. It was hard to believe they were made of stone. There were graceful statuaries everywhere, and lush gardens with shimmering pools and cascading fountains. Elves strolled in the gardens, talked together in small groups, or sat apart, reading or contemplating. Still others strummed lyres or trilled flutes while children danced. Music seemed a part of the air.

"Oh, how peaceful," Nell said breathlessly.

Xylon smiled. "We are fond of it," he said.

He led them to one of the closest buildings, stopped beside its tall, arched entrance, and rang a tinkling bell. Shortly a young female Elf appeared.

"Anana will look after your Dragons," said Xylon.

The girl came forward and stroked Beauty's neck. "What a beauty," she said. "What is her name?"

"You just said it," Nell replied. "It's Beauty."

"Ah," said the girl. "A perfect fit." She took the reins from Nell and Owen. "Fear not," she said. "I will care for them like my own."

Xylon turned to Zephy. "You know where to find the Elfsmith," he said. "The prince and princess must come with me."

"Why?" asked Zephy.

"The king and queen wish to meet them," said the Elf.

Nell and Owen exchanged surprised glances.

"How did they know we were coming?" Nell asked.

"The Elements have been astir for some time now," said Xylon. "This way, please."

He led them up to the castle, through a columned archway, and into a great courtyard garden. In the center of the garden was a gazebo-like structure with flowering vines twisting up and over it. Within this circular arbor sat the king and queen of Elvenlea.

The king looked much like Xylon, only a bit gray around the temples. His robes were also green, and he wore a crown of woven vines. The queen was dressed in a flowing gown of pale yellow. Her long blond hair was plaited all about her head, and a circlet of daisies sat upon her brow.

Xylon approached them and bowed.

"The Expected Ones are here, Majesties," he said.

Both of the royal Elves looked up with keen curiosity.

"Ah," said the king, "so these are the two we have heard so much about."

The queen beckoned Owen and Nell forward. "Come, my children."

Nell and Owen mounted the gazebo stairs and approached the thrones.

"I present King Ivor and Queen Ethelind," said Xylon.

Owen bowed and Nell, after a moment's hesitation, did the same. Curtsying in trousers just didn't seem natural.

"At your ease, my children," said the king. "If my instincts do not deceive me, you are of royal blood yourselves."

"Yes." Owen nodded. "We are Owen and Arenelle, prince and princess of Xandria."

"I sense that you have an important role to play in the future of Eldearth," said Queen Ethelind.

"We are both apprenticed to the Imperial Wizard," said Nell. "One of us may be the Promised One."

The queen pondered this a moment, then slowly shook her head. "No," she said. "I think not. The Magic is strong in each of you, it's true, but not strong enough, I fear."

Owen and Nell exchanged surprised glances.

"Certainly your intuitions are wrong," said Owen. "If neither of us is the Promised One, then who is?"

"This I cannot tell," said Queen Ethelind. "I can only tell that neither of you possess enough Magic to fulfill the destiny you seek."

Nell glanced down at the Charm Mark on her hand and over at Owen's. Was this why neither Charm Mark resembled the prophesized dove? Was there someone else? And if so, would the true Promised One appear in time to save Eldearth before it was too late?

"But, that can't be," Owen continued to argue.

Nell touched his arm.

"Owen," she said. "Whatever our destinies might be, we must return to the palace at once. We can use our powers to help defend the scepter, at least."

"Yes." Queen Ethelind nodded. "That would be wise."

But Owen's gaze was still riveted on the queen.

"But . . . we are still in training," he said. "We will get stronger in time."

"Time runs short," said King Ivor. "We have word that the Imperial Wizard lies on his deathbed, and Lord Taman pushes ever closer to the palace."

Nell's heart lurched.

"Lord Taman," Owen said contemptuously. "I thought we had seen the last of him."

"Whatever made you think that?" asked King Ivor.

"Last we saw him," said Owen, "he was fleeing for his life from a horde of angry Banshees."

"Well, he managed not only to escape, but to triumph," said Queen Ethelind. "Graieconn has appointed him Commander in Chief of all the Dark Forces, and Lord Taman has been sweeping relentlessly through kingdom after kingdom, driving all the armies of Eldearth before him."

Nell gasped. "What of the Castle Xandria?" she asked. "Have you word how Castle Xandria has fared?"

"I fear Castle Xandria has been razed and the surrounding village burned to the ground, as have most of the other villages of Eldearth."

Nell cried out and clasped a hand to her heart.

"How can this be?" she cried. "We have only been away from the castle a few days!"

"I'm sorry," said the king, "but our sources are quite reliable."

"Have you . . . any word of King Einar or Lady Fidelia?" Nell asked worriedly.

"No," said King Ivor. "But I have not heard that they are dead, so that is encouraging at least."

The word *dead* hit Nell in the face like a stinging blow. "We must return to the palace at once!" she cried to Owen.

Owen nodded gravely, then he turned back to King Ivor and Queen Ethelind.

"We are on the eve of an epic struggle," he said. "The skill of Elvish archers in feats of marksmanship is legendary. We could use your army by our side."

"I'm sorry," said Queen Ethelind, "but Elvenlea is a place of refuge and peace, a place for the furtherance of knowledge and the arts, not war. It has been our custom to remain neutral in the struggles of Eldearth."

"I fear you are mistaken if you think you can remain aloof from this war," said Owen. "If Graieconn wins, there will be no refuge, not even in Elvenlea."

King Ivor placed a hand on his wife's arm, and she looked up at him.

"The boy is right, my dear," he said. "Graieconn is no fool. He knows that education flies in the face of subjugation. If he would enslave Eldearth, his first task must be to destroy all centers of knowledge and culture."

The queen sighed heavily and rose from her chair. She walked to the edge of the gazebo and stood gazing out over the peaceful vistas of Elvenlea.

"I had hoped it would not come to this," she said. "I

have long had a dream that knowledge would win the race against evil, that those who visit here would take away with them the seeds of goodness—love, justice, mercy, respect—and that these would take root in Eldearth and flourish. I had hoped that the Light would one day shine of its own power again, even without the scepter."

Nell's heart quickened at the queen's words. It seemed that Nell's destiny suddenly made sense. Her purpose had became crystal clear.

"That is a lovely dream," said Owen, "but I'm afraid it belies the true nature of Folk."

Nell frowned. "No!" she declared. "I won't ever believe that. I can't."

"Well, believe it or not," said Owen. "It won't much matter if we don't win this battle. The race will be over."

"Then we *must* win," said Nell. She walked over, bowed before Queen Ethelind, and took her hand. "Help us," she said. "I believe that your dream can become reality, but we need time, much more time for the seeds of goodness to grow. For now we must pre-serve the scepter."

The queen rested a hand on Nell's head thoughtfully, then a quiet determination came into her eyes. She turned to King Ivor and solemnly nodded.

The king rose from his throne and put his hands out to Owen and Nell. "We are with you, our friends," he said.

# CHAPTER TWENTY-ONE

There could be no doubt that the Light was failing. The sky was as gray as dusk, clouded further with dust and smoke. The Legions of the Darkness would surely be able to move almost as efficiently in the day now as in the night, giving them a distinct advantage, since most of the Folk of Eldearth were helpless without light. If the tide didn't turn quickly, Graieconn himself would soon be free to roam Eldearth at will.

Nell, Owen, and Zyphyra began to see evidences of the war long before they came upon the battlefield. The swath of destruction was terrible, village after village burned to the ground, the land ravaged. Fallen soldiers and dead battle Dragons littered the ground. Here and there, ragtag groups of dispossessed Folk wandered as if in a daze, scrounging for food and shelter.

Nell's stomach was knotted in pain and fear. What if Lady Fidelia had been killed, or her father? She hadn't even spoken to him since their chilly parting over the question of the Bloodpox potion. Nell's faith in King Einar had been shaken. She had come to realize that his ideals had been forged in an age of ignorance and injustice, an age that was, one way or the other, passing away. She would never again blindly trust her father, but still, her love for him was unshakable. She couldn't bear to think that their heated words might have been the last they would ever speak to each other.

"There!" Owen suddenly shouted. "I see fires on the shores of that lake up ahead."

Nell peered through the gloom and saw the pinpoints of light that Owen was referring to. When they drew closer, the lights took the shape of cook fires on opposite sides of the lake. There seemed to be a lull in the fighting as both armies refueled themselves.

"Be careful," said Nell. "Don't get too close."

"Detour due west," said Owen. "We can fly low behind those hills and approach our army without being seen by Lord Taman's forces."

Owen's plan took them out of their way, but Nell had to agree that it was the only prudent way to get past the Dark Legions. As soon as they reached the far side of the lake they were confronted by two air guards on battle Dragons.

"Who goes there?" the guards demanded, pulling up alongside Beauty and Brahn.

"Princess Arenelle and Prince Owen of Xandria," said Nell.

"What is your business?" one of the guards asked.

"We bring news of reinforcements," said Nell. "A company of Elves is on its way."

"Elves!" the guards both exclaimed. "That is welcome news!"

"Can you tell us if there are Xandrian here?" Owen asked, "and if King Einar is leading them?"

"Yes on both counts," said one of the guards. "You'll find them down near the lakeshore on the easterly side."

Nell's heart swelled with joy. Her father was alive! Here! She turned Beauty in the direction that the guards had pointed and moments later she was on the ground amid a sea of the familiar purple uniforms of Xandria.

By the time Brahn landed, King Einar was already bursting through the crowd.

"Arenelle!" he cried, sweeping her up in his arms. "Ah, my precious jewel. What a feast for the eyes you are!"

Owen walked up and was quickly swept into the king's embrace as well.

"And my son, my son," he cried. "Thank the Scepter!"

The three laughed and cried and hugged for several minutes until Zephy finally cleared her throat loudly.

"Oh!" said Nell. "We forgot Zephy. Father, this is our dear friend and companion."

To her surprise, Zephy had to endure being swept up in the king's embrace as well.

"A dear friend of my children's is a dear friend of mine!" the king shouted.

"Hey!" came a familiar voice. "Can an old friend get in on this love fest?"

Nell whirled.

"Pim?" she called. "Is that you?"

"That it is!" came the voice again. "To your left and down!"

Nell swung her eyes left and lowered them. There was her old friend, standing on a log in front of the campfire! She reached down and Pim hobbled into her hand, leaning heavily on a cane. Nell brought him up close to her face.

"How are you, old friend?" she asked with a wide grin.

"Getting better every day," said Pim. "Won't be long till I can keep up with you again, Princess!"

"What a nice surprise to see you," Nell said.

"Got another old friend who might surprise you too," said Pim.

"Who?" asked Nell, looking around.

Pim pulled out a reed whistle and blew into it.

"You don't mean . . ." said Nell.

"I do," said Pim.

"Captain Treeleaper is here?" Nell asked in amazement.

"Yes, along with a full company of Hillkin warriors."

Nell glanced over at her father, chatting eagerly with Owen, then she leaned closer to Pim.

"How on Eldearth did you manage that?" she asked.

"I simply pointed out to your father," said Pim, "how advantageous it would be in this struggle to have some allies who are as comfortable in the darkness as Graieconn's forces."

"And the Hillkin were willing to fight with us?" said Nell in astonishment.

"Well, yes. Given certain concessions concerning the Montue trade," said Pim with a wry smile.

Nell grinned. "You never cease to amaze me, Pim," she said.

Just then Donagh Treeleaper came striding through the crowd of milling soldiers.

"Donagh!" cried Nell, running to meet her old friend.

"Princess!" said the Hillkin captain with a broad smile. He dipped his head. "Always a pleasure!"

"I am glad to see you well, Captain Treeleaper," said Nell, "and very glad to know that you and Father are allies now."

Donagh nodded. "We have come to an agreement that both of our peoples can live with," he said. Then his expression grew grave. "That is, if we come out of this battle alive."

"We will," said Nell. "We must."

"I fear I have some unhappy news in that regard," said Donagh.

Nell's brow wrinkled in concern. "What is it?" she asked.

"I regret to tell you that Lord Taman, whom you left in my custody, has escaped."

Nell sighed heavily. "I know," she said. "But you must not blame yourself. He has proven a far more wiley and worthy adversary than I ever imagined."

"Yes," said Donagh. "With his intimate knowledge of the inner workings of the kingdoms of Eldearth, he has been able to defeat us at every turn."

Owen and King Einar had joined the group.

"Would that we had killed him when we had the chance," Owen said.

"You had a chance to kill Lord Taman?" King Einar asked in surprise.

"Yes," said Nell remorsefully. "Back in Odom. It is my fault that we did not. I could not bring myself to do so."

The king nodded, his expression grave. "Understandable," he said. "He is your cousin after all, but . . ."

"I know," said Nell with a heavy sigh. "Not what a true leader would have done." She lowered her head, images of war and devastation flashing through her mind. Could she have helped prevent it all if her heart had just been a bit harder?

"Well, that is behind us now," said Owen. "We must concentrate on the task ahead. We bring good news: King Ivor and his archers are en route to join the fight."

"Elves!" said King Einar, his eyes widening. "That *is* welcome news. However did you convince them?"

"It did not take much convincing," said Owen.

"King Ivor understands the significance of this battle, as do we all."

King Einar nodded grimly, then turned and gazed across the plain where Folk of all kinds, friends and former foes, stood ready to fight side by side to defend the one thing they shared in common—Eldearth.

"As do we all," he murmured, then he turned back to the group. "If you will all excuse us," he said to Zephy, Pim, and Donagh, "there is a matter of some importance that I must discuss with my children."

Nell and Owen both looked at their father questioningly.

"Come," he said to them. "Walk with me by the lake. We know not how long these few moments of calm will last."

He slid an arm around each of their shoulders and guided them down along the shore. The lake sparkled peacefully in the pale moonlight. It was hard to believe that this serene place would soon be the scene of bloodshed and terror.

"I have news that may be difficult to hear," said King Einar.

Nell and Owen looked up into his face.

"It's Lady Fidelia," he said quietly.

Nell gasped and clutched her heart.

Owen went pale. "How . . . how bad?" he stammered.

The king shook his head in silent finality.

Nell felt iron claws close around her heart. Her legs

began to tremble and tears stung her eyes. She looked at Owen and saw his eyes were brimming with tears as well.

"Auntie," he whispered.

A sob burst from Nell's lips, and the tears spilled over and coursed down her cheeks.

King Einar pulled them both close and hugged them tightly.

"She was a brave Witch and a precious friend," he said. "She died fighting by my side."

Nell turned her face into her father's chest and let the sobs come.

"Why?" she whispered. "Why is the world so cruel?"

"I don't know, my jewel," said the king, "but you above all must not abandon hope. If despair claims your pure and valiant heart, then surely the rest of us are doomed."

Nell's heart didn't feel valiant. It felt battered and bloodied. She was tempted to give up. Why go on fighting? If Queen Ethelind was right about her and Owen, they were fighting in vain anyway. She was so tired . . . so tired. All she wanted to do was lay her weary head down somewhere, forget everything, and sleep.

Owen pulled away from King Einar's embrace and walked alone to the water's edge.

King Einar looked down at Nell. "Her last words

were for you, Nell," he said quietly. "She said to thank you."

Nell looked up. "Thank me? For what?"

"For showing her how strong she could be," he said.

Tears filled Nell's eyes again. "A lot of good that did," she cried. "It got her killed."

"Some things are worth dying for, Nell," said the king. "Lady Fidelia fought valiantly, defending Eldearth. She died a proud Witch."

Nell swallowed hard. She clutched her ruby pendant desperately. It grew warm and seemed to pulsate more powerfully than ever. Wherever her mother was, did she and Lady Fidelia stand hand in hand now?

"I love you both," Nell whispered. "And I will not give up." She squeezed her father's hand, then gently pulled away. She went to Owen and put a hand on his shoulder. He turned to look at her, tears shining bright in his eyes.

"We must fight all the harder now," she said quietly. "Lady Fidelia must not have died in vain."

Owen closed his eyes and squeezed out the tears. Then he opened them wide, clenched his jaw, and nodded.

Nell returned to her father's side. "Owen and I must go now," she told him. "We must return to the Keeper before it is too late."

King Einar sighed. "I fear to let you out of my sight in these terrible times," he said.

"And we fear to leave you," said Nell. "But I am glad to have had this reunion at least. Let us part in love this time, instead of in anger."

The king encircled his arms around Nell and hugged her tightly. "Love has always been ours, even in anger," he said, "but you are right. If part we must, let us at least have the memory of this embrace to hold in our hearts."

# Chapter Twenty-two

The sky was dark and stormy by the time Beauty and Brahn descended through the Lake of Illusion to the palace grounds. Nell was deeply worried—about the war, about her father, and about Queen Ethelind's unsettling premonition concerning the prophecy. If neither she nor Owen were meant to fulfill it, then who was, and where was this true Chosen One? Would he—or she—arrive in time?

Lady Aurora rushed out of the doors of the palace shortly after the Dragons touched down.

"Thank the Scepter you're all right!" she cried. "I was so worried! Oh, Zephy, what happened to your poor wings?"

"They'll heal," said Zephy. "There are more important things to worry about now."

"Yes, indeed," said Lady Aurora fretfully. She turned her attention to Nell and Owen. "The Keeper

is deathly ill, I'm afraid," she said. "He has been trying desperately to hold on until your return."

"Go to him," said Zephy to Owen and Nell. "I'll tend
to the Dragons."

"Speaking of Dragons," said Nell. "Where's Minna?"

"Come," said Lady Aurora with a mysterious smile.
"You'll be surprised."

Lady Aurora led them through the palace to the
Keeper's chambers. Quietly she pushed his door open.
The Imperial Wizard was reclining on a divan, his head
back, his eyes closed. Beside him in its stand, the
scepter glowed dimly. Curled up on his chest was a
sleeping Minna.

"Well, I'll be," said Nell.

"That's one sight I never thought I'd see," said
Owen.

Lady Aurora closed the door silently. "Are you both
such poor judges of character?" she asked. "Have you
not yet figured out that the Keeper's fuss and bluster is
all a show to hide the truth?"

"What truth?" asked Nell.

"That he is just a lonely old man, disappointed in
himself and disillusioned with Eldearth."

"Then why is he so mean to me?" asked Nell. "He
acts like he hates me."

"He doesn't hate you," said Lady Aurora. "He only
seeks to discourage you."

"But why?" asked Nell.

Lady Aurora glanced furtively at the closed door.

"You must promise never to tell him that I told you," she said.

Nell and Owen nodded.

"Long ago, when the Keeper was a young man, he had a wife and a daughter," said Lady Aurora.

"Imperial Wizards can marry?" said Owen.

"Of course," said Lady Aurora. "Why not?"

"I don't know," said Owen. "I just never pictured . . ."

"The Keeper was a devoted husband and father," said Lady Aurora. "His little girl was his heart's delight."

"What became of her?" asked Nell.

"When she was about your age," said Lady Aurora, "she and her mother were killed by Graieconn's henchmen, in the most brutal and terrible way."

Nell and Owen exchanged grim glances.

"He has always blamed himself," Lady Aurora went on, "because he wasn't strong enough to keep them safe."

"That's so sad," said Nell.

"Yes," said Lady Aurora. She pulled her wand out and pointed it at the wall. "Look," she said.

An image of a young girl appeared there.

"Is that her?" asked Nell.

Lady Aurora nodded.

"She . . . she looks like Nell," said Owen.

"Very much," said Lady Aurora. She lowered the wand and the image disappeared. "You remind him of her, Arenelle," she said. "That's why he is so hard on you. He wants to frighten you away. He fears for you."

Nell took in a deep breath and expelled it slowly. "Well, that would explain a lot," she said.

"Knowing this won't change anything," said Lady Aurora, "but I hope that it will enable you to have a bit more patience with him in his last days."

Nell nodded.

"Is he really so near to death?" asked Owen worriedly.

"I'm afraid so," said Lady Aurora. "Come now. He's been awaiting your return." She rapped lightly on the door, then pushed it open.

The Imperial Wizard opened his eyes and looked up, startled.

"Oh, oh!" he said, struggling to sit up. "You're back. It's about time!"

Minna tumbled into his lap and woke with a small cry. He looked down at her, pretending surprise.

"What are you doing here, you foolish worm?" he grumbled. "Lady Aurora, who let this pest in here?"

Lady Aurora looked over her shoulder at Nell and Owen and winked.

"Minna," called Nell. "Come."

"Thrummm!!" cried the little Demidragon, overjoyed to see Nell again. She zipped through the air and landed on Nell's shoulder, tickling the side of her face with little fork-tongued kisses.

"I missed you too," said Nell, reaching up to rub the nubby head.

The Wizard dissolved in a fit of coughing and had to lie down again.

"Where on Eldearth have you been?" he asked when he could speak.

"Trying to rescue Zephy," said Nell. She refrained from mentioning that Owen had required rescuing as well. He glanced at her with gratitude in his eyes.

The Wizard's brow furrowed. "And did you succeed?" he asked.

"Yes," said Nell. "She is wounded, but not seriously."

The Wizard's expression relaxed momentarily, then tensed with worry once more.

"How goes the war?" he asked.

"Not well," said Owen. "The Dark Forces are over-running Eldearth. We must revive the scepter."

The Wizard reached out and grasped the scepter with a trembling hand. It glowed slightly brighter, but seemed to sap all his remaining energy. He closed his eyes wearily.

"It is up to you now, boy," he said. "I have no more strength."

Nell and Owen exchanged glances.

"Go ahead," said Nell. "It doesn't matter."

Owen nodded and approached the scepter. He put out his right hand and grasped it tentatively. Nell could see his body jolt as a shock of energy flowed through him, but he held on, white-knuckled.

Nell, Lady Aurora, and the Wizard all stared at the scepter, willing it to glow even a little bit brighter, but there was no change.

"Concentrate, boy!" the Wizard bellowed. Then he fell into another fit of coughing.

Owen held his breath and fixed his eyes on the scepter, but it was in vain.

"Here," said Nell suddenly. She pulled the pendant up over her head and went over to Owen and slipped it over his head.

"Press it against your heart," she said.

Owen pressed against the pendant with one hand and clutched the scepter with the other.

Nell held her breath.

Nothing happened.

"It's no use," said the Wizard, his voice ragged and wheezy. "It's over."

"Not yet," said Owen. He let go of the scepter and stepped back. He removed the pendant and handed it back to Nell. "You try," he said.

The Wizard frowned. "No," he muttered.

Nell hesitated.

"Try!" Owen demanded.

Nell stepped forward and grasped the scepter. Its energy coursed through her, making her whole body tremble. Owen and Lady Aurora stared.

Nothing.

"The pendant," said Owen.

Nell grasped the pendant with her free hand and she could feel the energies bond, jerking her body violently.

But still nothing.

"Queen Ethelind was right," said Nell, letting go and stepping back, "neither of us are powerful enough."

The Wizard sighed heavily and grasped the scepter once more. "I tried," he whispered sadly. "I tried my best."

Suddenly there was a noise like thunder, and the whole palace shuddered. The scepter flickered.

"Keeper!" said Owen, rushing forward. "Hold on!"

"I can't," said the Imperial Wizard in a trembling voice. He seemed to be shriveling before their eyes. "The Darkness is coming. I can feel it."

Heavy pounding footsteps reverberated throughout the building, and then the chamber door flew open.

"Cousins!" said a booming voice. "We meet again."

# Chapter Twenty-three

"Who are you?" demanded Lady Aurora.

Lord Taman dipped his head with feigned courtesy.

"The name is Lord Taman," he said in a syrupy-sweet voice. "Commander in Chief of the armies of Darkearth!"

Lady Aurora went pale. "How did you come to this sacred place?" she asked.

"Sacred is in the eye of the beholder, my lady," said Lord Taman with a sneer. "This place holds no awe for me. And as for how I came here, you can blame your so-called Promised Ones for that."

"What are you talking about?" Nell challenged. "We had nothing to do with bringing you here."

"Bringing? No. Leading? Yes. You forget, dear cousin. That white Dragon of yours glows like a lamp in the night. My scouts saw you arrive at your father's camp, and when you left I was right behind you."

Nell swallowed hard. How could she have been so careless?

"It seems I've arrived just in time," Lord Taman went on.

"Just in time for what?" asked Nell.

"To take the scepter off your hands," said Lord Taman. "It would seem to be in need of a new master."

Nell and Owen both turned to look at the Imperial Wizard. He lay unmoving, but his hand still gripped the scepter, and the rod still glowed.

"I don't think so," said Owen. He stepped in front of the Wizard's couch. Nell moved to Owen's left and Lady Aurora to his right, forming a barrier between Lord Taman and the dying Keeper.

"How sweet," said Lord Taman.

"Take your wands out carefully," said Lady Aurora. "Hold them with all your strength."

Lord Taman laughed and extracted his own wand from his sleeve. He raised it and pointed it at Lady Aurora.

"Counter it!" shouted Lady Aurora.

Owen and Nell aimed their wands directly back at Lord Taman's. There was a sizzle of light and sparks flew from all four wands. A painful jolt burned up Nell's arm and she cried out involuntarily.

"Rrronk!" cried Minna. She launched herself off Nell's shoulder, directly at Lord Taman's wand, knocking it from his hand. Before he could retrieve it, she scooped it up and flew to the top of the window ledge.

"Good girl!" Nell shrieked.

"Oh, come now, Cousin," said Lord Taman. "Do you think I am still an amateur?"

He snapped his fingers, and Minna gave a startled cry and dropped the wand. It flew through the air, back to his waiting hand.

"Powers of Goodness, Powers of Light," Lady Aurora began to chant.

"All right, I've had about enough out of you," cried Lord Taman. He stood back and pointed his wand directly at Lady Aurora.

"Lord of Darkness," he intoned.

"He's trying to invoke Graieconn!" cried Lady Aurora. "Stop him!"

Nell and Owen both trained their wands on Lord Taman.

*Zap! Zap!* He turned this way and that, batting the beams of energy aside and sending them bouncing around the room. Each new volley sapped Nell and Owen of energy, but Lord Taman seemed unfazed.

*Zap! Zap! Zap!* Light zigged and zagged, back and forth. A searing jolt hit Nell's shoulder, numbing her arm. She dropped her wand, but immediately retrieved it with her other hand.

"Aagh!" cried Owen. A bolt of energy hit him dead in the chest and sent him staggering back against the wall. Breathing heavily, he righted himself and took aim again.

Lord Taman continued deflecting volley after volley, apparently unscathed.

"Aay!" cried Lady Aurora. Her wand clattered to the floor and she grabbed her hand. It was burned and twisted. "Aay!" she cried again as another burst hit her square in the forehead. She staggered backward and fell to the ground unmoving.

"Rrronk," cried Minna. She launched herself at Lord Taman once more, but got caught in the crossfire and fell screeching to the floor.

"Minna! Lady Aurora!" Nell cried, but there was no time to look after either of the fallen.

Lord Taman's volleys kept coming, and Nell and Owen took turns countering them, but each volley took its toll. Nell grasped her pendant with her injured hand. It gave her strength, but she was still no match for her evil cousin.

Another beam hit Owen hard in the chest and knocked the wind from his lungs. He fell to the floor gasping.

A zap hit Nell in the leg and her knee buckled. Then a zap blasted her wand from her hand and sent it skittering across the floor. She crawled after it, but just as she reached for the wand, a heavy boot pinned her hand to the floor.

She looked up into Lord Taman's defiant eyes.

"Well, that was a nice little diversion," he said haughtily. "Thank you all for the exercise. Now you and your brother, over there against the wall."

He lifted his boot and kicked Nell painfully in the side. She crawled over to Lady Aurora and Minna.

Lady Aurora was breathing, but unconscious. Minna whimpered in pain when Nell touched her, but at least she was alive.

"The wall I said!" Lord Taman boomed. He reached down and grabbed Owen by the neck, yanked him to his feet, and shoved him at the wall.

Owen hit the wall hard and tumbled to the floor. Nell dragged herself over to his side.

Lord Taman stomped over and glared down at them.

"Well, kiddies, the game is over," he said, "and guess who won?"

Nell looked up at him in bewilderment.

"Can you just tell me one thing?" she asked.

"Depends," said Lord Taman. "What?"

"Why?" asked Nell.

Lord Taman threw his head back and laughed.

"Haven't we had this conversation before?" he asked. "Power, my naïve little cousin. It's always about *power*."

"But you *had* power," said Nell. "You were the Grand Court Wizard of Xandria."

"I don't want to be Grand Court Wizard," he said. "I want to be king, like my grandfather, and why shouldn't I be? My mother was his oldest child."

"But your mother was . . ." Nell hesitated.

"Was what?" said Lord Taman with a cynical smile. "A woman? How ironic! Aren't you the Witch who wants to be a Wizard? Are you telling me you think it's fair that the throne should pass right over my mother just because she was a woman?"

"Well, I . . ."

"Hypocrite!" cried Lord Taman, pointing a finger right at Nell's nose.

Nell stared at the hand in front of her face and gasped.

"By the Light!" she blurted. "The Mark of the Dove!"

# Chapter Twenty-four

"Owen, look!" Nell cried.

Owen struggled to sit up. He stared at Lord Taman's hand.

"That's not a Charm Mark," he said. "It's Graieconn's sign with a scar under it!"

"I know," said Nell, "but think about it. The prophecy doesn't really mention a Charm Mark. It just says the Mark of the Dove!" She grabbed Lord Taman's hand and turned it so Owen could get a better look. "The scar is the body, don't you see," she said, "and the cloven hoof forms the wings."

"What are you two blathering about?" asked Lord Taman, yanking his hand away.

"You . . . you bear the Mark of the Dove," Nell stammered. "You could be the Chosen One!"

"Have you lost your mind?" snapped Owen. "He's no more the Chosen One than Graieconn is."

Nell chewed her lip, her thoughts in a jumble. Surely

one as evil as Lord Taman couldn't be the Chosen One. Or could he? Perhaps there was still some good in him. Perhaps he could yet be saved.

"Think about the prophecy, Owen," she said. "*Royally born, tragedy torn.* Those things apply to Lord Taman as much as they do to us. . . . Plus he's already a powerful Wizard *and* he bears the Mark of the Dove–"

"It's a scar and a cloven hoof," Owen interrupted.

"It's still a dove," said Nell. "And he has found the Palace of Light."

"By following us," said Owen.

"And you found it by stealing a Dragon," Nell pointed out.

Lord Taman was listening to them with interest.

"Are you telling me," he said at last, "that you think *I* am destined to be the next Imperial Wizard?"

Nell stared hard at her cousin's face, searching for some sign of repentance, some small glimmer of goodness. "I think you *could* be," she said.

"No!" cried Owen.

"Why not?" asked Nell.

"He's a traitor and a heartless murderer," said Owen. "He'll stop at nothing to get what he wants!"

"Maybe that's because he's felt cheated and wronged all his life," said Nell.

"Hey, he had it a lot better than I did," said Owen, "and I didn't sell my soul to Graieconn."

"Maybe you're just blind to the truth because you

don't want to admit that he might be the Chosen One instead of you," said Nell. "You want the power yourself."

"I do not," said Owen. "You're the one who's blind to the truth. You're letting your heart rule your head."

Nell took a deep breath.

"Well, have you got another explanation for the prophecy?" she asked.

Owen had no answer.

"Now, let me make sure I've got this right," said Lord Taman. "You"—he pointed at Nell—"think that I"—he thumped his chest—"should be the Keeper of the Scepter?"

Nell sucked in a deep breath and squared her shoulders. "Yes," she said.

"No!" cried Owen. "Nell, think of what you're saying. You can't believe that we should put the scepter in his hands!"

"I'm sorry, Owen," said Nell, "but it *has* to be him. It's the only answer." She looked up at Lord Taman. "Will you take it?" she asked.

Lord Taman stared at her a long time.

"I am deeply touched," he said at last, "by your sense of fair play and your faith in me. Perhaps I have been misguided. Yes. I will take the scepter, Cousin, as you wish."

Nell smiled thinly. Was he sincere? Had she made the right choice?

"No," said Owen firmly. He scrambled to his feet,

but Lord Taman was already across the room, reaching for the scepter. There was a flash of light when he touched it. His eyes went wide and his hand trembled. His whole body jerked, but he did not let go.

Owen held his breath.

Nell stared, willing for the scepter to glow.

Instead it grew fainter.

"Oh no," she whispered.

Lord Taman lifted the scepter over his head and shook it triumphantly in the air. "I will take it all right!" he yelled. "I will take it straight to Graieconn!"

Owen hurled himself across the room and lunged for the scepter, but Lord Taman deftly stepped aside, and Owen crashed hard into the wall and crumpled to the floor. Lord Taman grasped the scepter with both hands like a sword. He lifted it high, preparing to plunge it into Owen's heart!

"No!" Nell screamed. She jumped to her feet and flew at Lord Taman. She grabbed hold of the scepter and a numbing jolt of power coursed through her body, but she held on desperately.

"No," she cried. "Don't hurt him! Please! Think about what you're doing!"

Lord Taman yanked the scepter up, ripping it from Nell's hands, then he brought it down like a club and bashed her in the chest, sending her reeling backward and crashing to the floor. She lay helpless, gasping for breath as he once again raised the scepter over Owen's inert body and prepared to drive it through his heart.

"Nooo!" Nell screamed, her voice strangled.

And then there was a brilliant flash of light. Lord Taman screamed. His back went rigid and he staggered backward. The scepter fell clattering to the floor. Lord Taman stood a moment longer, immobile, his arms still raised above his head and then he fell crashing to the floor and lay unmoving, his eyes staring glassily at the ceiling, his face fixed in an expression of surprise.

Nell dragged herself to her knees and crawled over to him. She put a hand to his heart. It was still.

There was a wracking cough and she turned to see the Imperial Wizard propped up on one elbow, his wand in his hand.

"Keeper!" she said in a hushed voice. "You . . . you killed him. You saved the scepter!"

A satisfied smile spread across the old Wizard's face, then he collapsed, and the scepter went dark.

# CHAPTER TWENTY-FIVE

There was a terrible roar and the palace began to shake. There was not a glimmer of light anywhere.

"Owen," cried Nell. "Where are you?"

"Oooh," moaned Owen.

"Owen!" Nell scrambled over to the sound. "Owen, are you all right?"

Wind howled and thunder rumbled and the palace began to creak and crack.

"What . . . what's happening?" Owen groaned.

"Lord Taman is dead, and so is the Keeper," said Nell.

"Graieconn," said Owen. "He'll be coming for the scepter."

"By the Light," Nell said in a whimper. "I'm such a fool."

"No time for that now," said Owen. "We've got to save the scepter."

"How?" asked Nell.

There was a violent shudder and the sound of shattering glass.

"The palace is breaking apart," said Owen. "We've got to get out of here."

"Owen! Nell!" came a plaintive voice. "Where are you?"

"Here, Zephy!" yelled Owen. "In the Wizard's bedchamber!"

There was the sound of running footsteps, and then Zephy burst into the room.

"I can't see anything," she said.

"The scepter has gone out," said Owen. "Graieconn is coming and the palace is falling. We've got to get out of here."

"What of the Wizard and Lady Aurora?" asked Zephy.

"The Wizard is dead," said Owen, "and Lady Aurora is hurt. Come help me carry her. Nell, you take Minna and the scepter."

Nell got to her feet and, cradling Minna in one arm, felt her way across the room with the other. At last she reached Owen.

"Here," he said, handing her the scepter. It felt strangely cold and still.

Owen and Zephy each took one of Lady Aurora's arms. She moaned as they started carefully dragging her across the room. The palace lurched again, and they huddled in the doorway momentarily while great shards of glass crashed around them.

"We've got to pick her up," said Owen. "She'll be cut to ribbons if we drag her."

Owen put his arms under Lady Aurora's and Zephy took her legs.

"Lead the way," said Owen to Nell. "We'll follow the sound of your footsteps."

Nell stumbled out into the hall and lurched down the corridor as the building rocked and shuddered, glass crashing everywhere. A great shard grazed her shoulder and another nicked her arm. Minna whimpered and Nell hugged her closer.

"Are you doing all right?" Nell asked over her shoulder. "I can take a turn carrying her."

"No, she's not that heavy," said Owen. "We're managing."

At last they reached the throne room in the heart of the palace. The wind was roaring through gaping holes in the ceiling now, and horrible sounds filled the air, like the wailing of a million tormented souls.

Nell stubbed her toe into a chair and tumbled over it. The scepter clattered to the ground and rolled away.

Suddenly the roaring of the wind reached an earsplitting pitch and the rotting stench of death filled the room.

"He's here!" Owen said, gasping. "He's on the doorstep."

"The scepter!" Nell cried. "I've dropped it!"

"You what!" Owen sounded exasperated. "Where? Where are you?"

"Here!" Nell laid Minna on the chair, and crawled across the floor, feeling for the scepter. Broken glass cut painfully into her hands and knees, but she didn't care.

"I've got it!" she cried at last.

"No, I've got it," said Owen right behind her. "You go help Zephy. I can't trust you with it."

"Yes, you can," Nell said, refusing to let go. "I'll be more careful. I swear."

"No," said Owen stubbornly. He grabbed hold of the scepter and they struggled for a moment, tugging back and forth.

"Give it to me!" yelled Owen.

"No!" Nell held tight. "I can handle it!"

Then there was a flicker of light. Then a dull glimmer. The scepter had begun to glow!

It grew warmer and brighter until Owen and Nell found themselves staring into each other's eyes.

The wind stilled and the palace stopped shaking. The wailing grew louder and louder, twisting into a horrible earsplitting screech of pain. Then it slowly died away, taking the stench with it.

The scepter glowed ever more brightly. Nell stared at it in astonishment.

"Owen, look," she whispered.

Owen looked down. Where their hands touched, on the shaft of the scepter, their Charm Marks met, forming the Mark of the Dove.

# CHAPTER TWENTY-SIX

Nell and Owen flew side by side on Beauty and Brahn. Minna fluttered proudly between them. Below, Elvenlea was green and beautiful. Flowers nodded and trees swayed in the balmy breeze. Colorful flags flew from hundreds of tents. Contingents from nearly every kingdom on Eldearth had come to witness the ceremony—the dawning of the New Chilead, the crowning of the new Keepers.

The crowds cheered as the beautiful Dragons set down. Nell and Owen dismounted and walked toward each other. They joined hands and began the long walk down the white carpet to where two identical thrones waited, one on either side of the shimmering scepter.

Nell was dressed all in white, except for the little Demidragon that sat like a bright purple corsage on her shoulder, and the ruby red pendant around her neck. She wore a dress of shimmering brocade, her hair caught up and twined with pearls. Lady Fidelia would have smiled approvingly and told her she was beautiful. It was a day to be beautiful.

Friends reached out to Nell and Owen as they walked by, and Nell took each and every hand.

"Pim," she said, "Lady Aurora and Zephy, dear Zephy . . . Donagh! Gurit! Miette! And Saidi! Oh my! Talitha! Leah! And my goodness—Orson! Who would have thought?"

So many friends, so many blessings. It was hard to keep the tears from spilling down her cheeks.

At last they reached the throne platform, and the trumpeters announced the beginning of the formalities.

Together they mounted the steps, then smiled at each other and turned to face the crowd. So many upturned faces. So many expectations. Nell hoped that she and Owen were up to the task before them. There were kingdoms to rebuild, lives to repair, injustices to fight, wrongs to be made right. It would not be easy, but they had a lifetime ahead of them and good friends to lend a hand.

King Einar came forward with Queen Ethelind on his left and King Ivor on his right. The Elf monarchs bore two identical crystal star-shaped circlets on pillows of white satin. King Einar beamed at his children. He reached out a hand to each of them.

"Would that your mother were here to see this day," he said.

Nell touched her gleaming pendant, and Owen rested a hand on the dagger in his belt.

"She is," they both said softly.

King Einar nodded and squeezed their hands.

"Have you decided who shall be crowned first?" he asked quietly.

"Yes," said Owen. "We flipped a coin, and I won."

"And that is satisfactory to you?" King Einar asked Nell.

"Perfectly," she answered.

The king smiled. "Your first official compromise," he said. "It bodes well." Then he turned to face the crowd.

"It is my distinct honor," he said, "to present to you the new Keepers of the Scepter!"

The crowd cheered wildly.

King Einar took the circlet from King Ivor and placed it on Owen's head. "Owen of Xandria," he said, "do you profess to protect the scepter?"

"I do," said Owen. "With all my power as Imperial Wizard!"

King Einar then took Nell's circlet into his hands. He placed it on her head. "Arenelle of Xandria," he said, "do you profess to protect the scepter?"

"I do," said Arenelle. "With all my power as Imperial . . . *Witch*."

King Einar and Owen both looked at her.

"What?" King Einar asked.

"I choose to be known as Imperial Witch," Nell said simply.

"But . . . I thought you were determined to become a Wizard," said King Einar.

"Why?" asked Nell. "When Witches are the equals of Wizards in every way?"

There was a silence, and then Queen Ethelind stepped forward. "Why indeed?" she said with a smile. She took Owen's left hand and Nell's right hand and joined them above her head. "Long live the Keepers!" she shouted. "Long live our Imperial Witch and Wizard!"

"Long live the Keepers," the crowd repeated. "Long live our Imperial Witch and Wizard!"

The trumpets blared and the cheering went on and on.

King Einar smiled, love shining in his eyes. "Indeed," he said.

"Thrummm!" hummed little Minna.

And the scepter shone upon them all, great and small.

# ABOUT THE AUTHOR

JACKIE FRENCH KOLLER is the author of more than thirty books for children and young adults, including the popular Dragonling fantasy series, available in a two-volume collector's set. Her books have garnered numerous awards and honors from the American Library Association, the International Reading Association, and many others, and have been published in several foreign languages. One of her novels was made into the movie *You Wish* for the Disney Channel. Ms. Koller, mother of three grown children, now lives on a mountain in western Massachusetts with her husband, George, and her black Lab, Cassie. She welcomes visitors to her Web site: http://www.jackiefrenchkoller.com.

Don't miss all the titles in this exciting fantasy adventure!

# THE KEEPERS

## By Jackie French Koller

### Can Nell complete the dangerous quest?

In the magical world of Eldearth, Witches and Wizards live side by side with Humans. Weefolk, though elusive, are abundant, and Dragons and Unicorns still walk the land. But the present Imperial Wizard, Keeper of the Light that protects Eldearth, is ill. If a new Apprentice is not found soon, Eldearth may succumb to the evil powers of the dark Lord Graieconn. There is a long tradition in Eldearth that the Keeper must be a Wizard, and only boys can be Wizards, but so far, all the boys who have attempted the difficult quest to become Apprentice Keeper have failed. Princess Arenelle, a promising young Witch, has just reached eleven, the age of Magic, and wishes to undertake the quest. She sets out with her pet Demidragon, Minna, on an adventure that will turn her world upside down. Everything she has ever believed will be challenged. Everything she has ever loved will be endangered, and the powers of Good and Evil will assume the most unexpected forms and faces. Does Nell have the wisdom, the courage, and the heart to meet her destiny? The future of Eldearth hangs in the balance!

**BOOK ONE:**

**BOOK TWO:**

**BOOK THREE:**

## Available from Aladdin Paperbacks

She's sharp.

She's smart.

She's confident.

She's unstoppable.

And she's on your trail.

**MEET THE NEW NANCY DREW**

Still sleuthing,

still solving crimes,

but she's got some new tricks up her sleeve

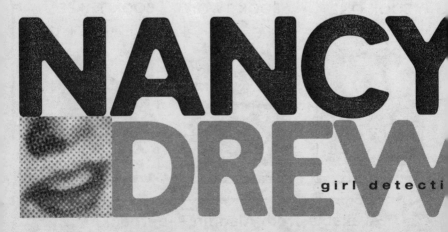

# NANCY DREW

girl detecti